Ashley Ladd

CIVIL AFFAIRS

ELLORA'S CAVE
ROMANTICA PUBLISHING

D1525855

An Ellora's Cave Romantica Publication

www.ellorascave.com

Civil Affairs

ISBN #1419952080
ALL RIGHTS RESERVED.
Civil Affairs Copyright© 2004 Ashley Ladd
Edited by: Briana St. James
Cover art by: Syneca

Electronic book Publication: December, 2004
Trade paperback Publication: June, 2005

Excerpt from *American Beauty* Copyright © Ashley Ladd, 2003
Excerpt from *Carbon Copy* Copyright© Ashley Ladd, 2004

Warning:

The following material contains graphic sexual content meant for mature readers. *Civil Affairs* has been rated *E-rotic* by a minimum of three independent reviewers.

Ellora's Cave Publishing offers three levels of Romantica™ reading entertainment: S (S-ensuous), E (E-rotic), and X (X-treme).

S-*ensuous* love scenes are explicit and leave nothing to the imagination.

E-*rotic* love scenes are explicit, leave nothing to the imagination, and are high in volume per the overall word count. In addition, some E-rated titles might contain fantasy material that some readers find objectionable, such as bondage, submission, same sex encounters, forced seductions, etc. E-rated titles are the most graphic titles we carry; it is common, for instance, for an author to use words such as "fucking", "cock", "pussy", etc., within their work of literature.

X-*treme* titles differ from E-rated titles only in plot premise and storyline execution. Unlike E-rated titles, stories designated with the letter X tend to contain controversial subject matter not for the faint of heart.

Civil Affairs

Chapter One

Paige Forbes eyed her post office box at the University of Southern Mississippi with trepidation. *Would Danny answer her?* It had been over a month since she'd mailed her letter to him. *How long did the military take to post mail to Baghdad? What if Danny was in the midst of battle? What if he was dead...*

No! Tormented by her melancholy thoughts, she chided herself for fearing the worst. She had been in love with Danny Napolitano just about forever, since before she had braces, before she understood what real love was, and even through the miserable days when he and her older brother, Jimmy, had taken demented delight in teasing her unmercifully about her freckles galore. Even throughout the long, tortuous years he had gone steady with Penny Foster, the high school cheerleading captain.

Danny probably thought of her as Jimmy's plump, dorky kid sister. Why should he waste a precious postage stamp on her?

Still, she stared hopefully at the silvery steel box, afraid to find it empty yet again or, worse, housing a return reply of '*Paige who?*'. Several students jostled her on their way to find their own dreams-come-true-in-an-envelope. Annoyed, she knew she wasn't even close to being invisible but, the way people always cut in front of her, it sure made her wonder.

Tax accounting class started in half an hour across campus in the business epicenter so she didn't have all day to stand there like an idiot unless she wanted her accounting prof to make an example of her coming in late yet again. The wicked man delighted in persecuting ill-fated students.

Sucking in her breath, she steeled herself for yet more disappointment and opened the box. *Glory be!* There it was, an envelope with an APO return address.

She withdrew it with shaky fingers, her gaze never leaving it lest it was a cruel trick of her imagination and would evaporate into nothingness. But her fingers slid across the very tangible and crumpled paper, and the paper hissed when she ripped it open.

Excitement soared through her veins and she held her breath as she unfolded the long-awaited answer praying it would be kind. Disappointed that there was a mere sheet without much scrawl, she consoled herself that he had answered.

Absconding with her treasure to a deserted corner of the Student Union, she sank to the floor and crossed her legs Indian-style. Then she hunkered down happily to read Danny's reply.

"Dear Paige,

Thanks for writing to me. God I miss everybody at home. I was sure surprised to hear my name at Mail Call. Some guys get letters from their folks and sweethearts almost daily but I guess Mom, Dad and Claire aren't much in the way of writers.

I didn't think anyplace on earth could be this hot but then this is Hell's Backyard. There's not much to do here except drill, fight and sweat.

Slop would be good compared to what the army calls food. I've lost at least fifteen pounds between not eating and all the marching.

Jimmy had mentioned that you're in college. What classes you taking? I sure miss USM. Never thought I'd end up in the African desert while I was sitting in economic lectures.

Good to hear from you. Hope you write again.

Danny"

Paige reread the letter a dozen times. An epistle it wasn't but it was friendly enough on the surface. Loneliness echoed between the lines, however, and she blinked rapidly, unexpected heartache eating at her. Had everyone, even his family, forgotten him?

He deserved far better. Firm resolve buoyed her spirits and she thrust out her chin determined that she would write to him as long as he didn't reject her.

Her legs tingled, having fallen asleep as she'd pored over his letter several times. When the Student Union grew abnormally quiet, she checked her watch and gasped. *Seven minutes to class. Great!* Her heart skipped several beats. She'd have to sprint to make it and that wouldn't be easy hauling an armload of books plus her own excess seventy pounds.

She slipped into the graduate class just in time to avoid humiliation but her heart wasn't in the lecture. Her jumbled thoughts kept straying from the lesson, which droned on unbearably. Visions of Danny in his dusty, sweaty fatigues teased her and her knees went weak. Drawing his name with flowery flourishes in the margin of her accounting notes, she longed for the mind-numbing class to end so she could whip off a reply.

Finally, her prof ended his sleep-inducing lecture, dropping a hint about a pop quiz sometime in the next week. Free at long last, she escaped into the blazing Delta sunshine. Much too gorgeous a day to hole up in her dorm room, she dumped her books on her bed and escaped outside again where she stretched out beneath a quiet palm tree by the lake. The twittering birds sounded so much prettier than her roommate's soap operas that she considered camping out there permanently.

Leaning against the tree trunk, her knees tucked up as a writing board, she chewed the end of her pen. Gazing into the hazy distance as she watched a butterfly twitter around, she wondered if it was day or night in Baghdad. *What was Danny doing? Did he ever think of her? Did he pine for Penny? Or had he met some cute little soldier in his platoon?*

Grimacing, she tried to push her disturbing musings aside. Putting pen to paper, she started several letters just to scrap them. Dull and pathetic, her words were stilted. Did she want to announce that her life was boring? Overweight accounting majors usually got left behind in the university library every weekend, while their prettier, slimmer roommates worked on obtaining their MRS degrees, but Danny didn't need know that.

Or was it that the only MRS degree she wanted was attached to Danny's last name? *How pathetic!* Would Danny cringe she was fantasizing about him? Why would he want her when stunning beauties like Penny flocked to him?

Still, she would be his moral support for as long as he was serving his country and defending her freedom several time zones away from home. It was the least she could do from here in paradise, where her toes wriggled in the springy grass, the soft breeze kissed her cheeks and dragonflies entertained her with their lazy air ballet.

"Dear Danny,

From the address, you can see I'm still at USM.

I'm a graduate student taking fifteen hours. Penny put in a good word for me so I'm working with her part-time in the University bookstore in the accounts receivable department. Experience for the resume...

Studying and work keep me pretty busy but I'm trying to walk and watch what I eat.

Have you seen any action? What's it like over there? Will you be coming home soon?

Paige"

A million questions clamored to be asked but she thought it best not to bombard the poor guy with her rampant curiosity. She wanted to know all about his days...and nights...but that would be much too forward.

* * * * *

One sandy, dreary day lolled into the next. It was so dry the trees were bribing the dogs and the only precipitation he could count on was the perspiration glistening on his own brow. Leaner and meaner than five months ago, when he'd first been stationed in this loathsome desert, he wasn't the same man who had left Biloxi.

During dinner he read Paige's second letter. By now the envelope was deeply creased and crumpled from having lived in his pocket since Mail Call. Charmed by the redhead's sweetness and humor, he chuckled.

"Dear Danny,

I worry about you over there. I watch the news with my heart in my throat.

When I get stressed out about my classes and work, I think how easy I have it compared to you.

What is it like? Truly?

Hang in there. Any word on when you get to come home yet? I hope it's before Halloween. At least before Christmas.

Hopefully I'll lose a size or two by then.

Love,

Paige"

More sweat on his brow than usual, he reread the part about Paige wanting to lose a couple sizes by the time he went home. *She wanted to look nice for him?* He was flattered. More than flattered, he was downright pleased. Too much so for his peace of mind.

So the pretty little redhead was still sweet on him? Her adolescent crush had almost been embarrassing. By now he thought she would have forgotten all about that. A graduate student, she should be on a dating orgy and have long since forgotten all about him.

He'd not seen her since he left for college. On the rare occasion he'd come home to visit, she'd been out of town. Surely she'd lost her braces and Pippi Longstocking pigtails by now. No way could she lose all those freckles. One of his greatest pastimes had been teasing her about her solid mass of freckles. But he had kept to himself how her creamy jade eyes reminded him of sultry summer nights and spoke of her promising womanhood still to blossom. With her striking coloring, she had the potential to grow up into a beauty one day and he wondered if that day had come? She must be what now? Twenty-five? Twenty-six?

He wished he had a current picture of her to see how she'd turned out.

"Since when were you anti-social, Napoleon?" His buddy, Rocco Pizzino from the Bronx, stretched out beside him, opening his MRE. He sniffed and wrinkled his nose at the military dinner. "Dog food'd taste better than this crapola."

"It's definitely not my mama's home cooking." Danny checked around him carefully and, when he saw that no one was paying attention, he took out four pieces of red licorice and tossed two to his buddy. "Merry Christmas. Don't say I never gave you nothing."

Rocco's eyes widened. Practically salivating, he attacked the red sticks as if he hadn't eaten in weeks.

"You're so pathetic. My hound dogs don't devour grub that fast," Danny drawled in his thick southern accent.

Rocco scowled at him. "Yo! What's pitiful is what the army tries to pass over on us for grub. When I get home, I'm treating myself to the juiciest, thickest Porterhouse steak at the best restaurant in the Bronx. I don't care if it costs two paychecks."

Without warning, Rocco leaned forward and snatched Paige's letter from Danny's hand. "Napoleon's got a Marie Antoinette. You been holding out on me. Spill, brother."

Danny dove for the private letter, not wanting his friend's grubby hands all over it. "Give it back." He growled, surprised at his fierce reaction, as if the dude dared flirt with his woman. "She's just a friend."

Disappointment flickered across Rocco's eyes as he read the letter. He must have expected something a lot more risqué. Then shrewdness flashed across his eyes. "Does she have a boyfriend?"

Protective instincts welled up in him. He'd trust his friend with his life, but not with an innocent young woman, even on paper. "Why?" Truth is, he didn't know.

"Seeing she's not your old lady, maybe she could write to me, too? Or maybe she has a friend who wants a pen pal?" The glint in Rocco's eyes told Danny that he was more ravenous for a pen pal than he had ever been for the licorice. Of course women were in the forces now so they weren't exactly starved for feminine companionship but it was difficult to see their beauty when covered in desert sands and sweat.

"You think I'd let you loose on some innocent woman? Think again." Danny plucked his booty out of his friend's grasp.

"Oh come on. You know what it's like not to get any mail." He stared off into the distance, holding his knees. "At least until your new friend started writing to you. I'm harmless."

No matter how much his buddy whined, he wasn't getting his paws near Paige or her letters. "I'll see if she has a friend who's interested in being pen pals. No promises." *What was he? A dating service?* He shook a finger at his buddy. "You keep this to yourself or the deal's off."

"Coppice." Rocco rose to his feet, stretched toward the sky and grinned down at him. Excitement blazed from his eyes.

Danny hoped he didn't look so pitiful over the prospect of a girl. Anyone looking at his friend would think he hadn't sniffed the scent of a female in years, instead of a few months.

Not 'til a couple of hours later, when they were bedding down for the night in their encampment, did Danny find the chance to write back to Paige. He traded a few pieces of licorice for writing paper and a stamp. The red stuff was better barter than money in this neck of the woods.

He zipped his sleeping bag around him, pulled it over his head and used his flashlight as a lamp. He'd never been one to write much of anything but he found it easy to write to Paige. His pen couldn't move fast enough to keep up with the words that poured forth from his mind.

"Dear Paige,

Getting your letter was better than eating red licorice. My friend Rocco stole it but I fought him for it. Before I forget, he wants to know if you have any single girlfriends that want to write to him. He's a short and scrappy little Italian from the Bronx but he's a good guy. He's saved my neck a few times. I told him no promises.

You're trying to lose weight? It's sweet that you want to do it for me. What have you done to try to lose it? Walking's one of the best ways. Or try eating this slop. If not for my stash of red licorice, I'd have starved long ago.

You still have all those freckles and pigtails? Please send me a RECENT picture of yourself. Here's one of me that the guys took not too far outside of Baghdad.

If it's not too forward, may I ask you to send some stamps, envelopes and writing paper so I can write back to you?

Good luck with your diet.

Love,

Danny"

He had a compelling desire to seal the letter with a kiss, but stopped himself. *Hello! This was Paige, the girl next door. His best friend's little sister.* So he sealed it, addressed it and dropped it in the mailbox before it fell out of his pocket.

A grenade exploded a few feet away, knocking Danny face first into the sand.

Battered, spewing sand from his mouth, Danny crawled to the safety of a tank and took cover behind its massive steel body.

"Take cover! Arm yourselves!" he yelled to his men.

Bombs burst, lighting the night sky, illuminating the high spiral minarets of mosques and palaces. If not so deadly, the light show brightening the city would be breathtaking. But the gunpowder reeked of death and he gritted his teeth as he rammed the safety off his weapon.

What he wouldn't give to resume a normal life, away from the stench of death and destruction. If he could remember what that was anymore. Would he ever return to normal?

The only link to normal he possessed was Paige's letter tucked in his pocket. That, and his nearly depleted cache of candy.

Gunfire rained on his platoon and Rocco, who was manning the machine gun, clutched his shoulder, whimpered and slumped to the side in slow motion.

"No!" Danny let loose a warrior's scream, his heart pounding so hard against his ribs they were bruised and battered. Frightened for his friend, he crawled on his belly to the soldier's side as he dodged a shower of M-16 rifle fire, and pulled the burly man to the safety of cover.

The blood staining Rocco's fatigues, combined with his shallow breathing, scared Danny far more than enemy fire ever could. "Hang in there, bubba. You're too mean to die on me."

Rocco's smile wavered and his ebony lashes fluttered over his pasty cheeks. "Yeah, only the good die young. Guess you'll never kick the bucket."

"Nor will you." Danny ripped his friend's torn shirt off his shoulder and applied pressure to the nasty wound to stanch the steady flow of blood until help arrived. He bellowed, "Man down! We need a medic over here."

War's basic horrors struck Danny square in the chest. He'd been through it all before over the past few months, except now it was trying to claim one of his buddies. The hostilities wore thin on him, and he cradled Rocco in his arms as he promised, "Hang on, bubba. We'll get you out of here and fixed up better than new."

He breathed a sigh of relief when a humvee rushed to their side. "The docs are here. They're going to medevac you out of this hellhole."

Rocco's weak smile slipped. Gasping, he mumbled, gritting his teeth, "Guess your girlfriend's friend can write to me at the hospital. I'm going to miss your ugly mug. Make sure you avoid these sons of bitches… They hurt like hell."

"I'll do my best." Choked up but wanting to put on a brave front for his friend, Danny couldn't squeeze another word from his throat.

"I don't want to die in this godforsaken furnace. Let me die on American soil, with some dignity." A tear squeezed from Rocco's eye, trailing down his swarthy cheek.

Danny bit his tongue hard and gritted his teeth until he could get control of his spiraling emotions. "You're not going to die." He hoped he wasn't lying. The wound looked too high to have pierced his heart but he was an accountant, not a physician.

Rocco squeezed Danny's fingers with a fraction of his normal strength as the medics inserted an IV in his arm. His fingers remained curled around Danny's until his stretcher was lifted into the medical unit.

Revenge was a bitch! Those enemy bastards would wish they had never been born than mess with his good pal.

Chapter Two

Paige could wear out the best scholars studying. Unfortunately, she couldn't seem to do it without chowing down on a bag of M&M's or chips, except at the library. Her lack of willpower distressed her, but the sadder, more stressed-out she became, the more she munched out. And she was putting on pounds instead of losing them, despite popping diet pills that were supposed to curb her appetite.

On the long shot she ever saw Danny again, or rather that he would see her, she wanted to be trim and svelte, not carrying around a second person in the same body.

"You're never going to get your MRS if you keep sticking your nose in books twenty-four-seven," Paige's best friend, Tia Reid, said in a sing-song voice as she dropped her stack of texts on the library table across from Paige. They made a loud bang, attracting several hostile glares to which Tia seemed oblivious.

Paige downed another diet pill and chased it with a swig of bottled water and grimaced. Then she flipped to the next page of her oh-so-exciting tax accounting workbook. "Like you're one to talk. When's the last time you went out on a date? Besides, women don't come to college to find a husband, they come to find their bridesmaids."

"Bite me." Tia flipped her gorgeous mane of silky onyx hair behind her shoulders and flopped into the ladder-back wooden chair. She studied her manicured nails carefully. "It's not like I can't get a date if I want. I'm just not in a hurry. Quality, not quantity, darling."

Uh-huh. Half-Polynesian, half-Latino, Tia was the most exotic woman on campus. Men trailed her around begging for dates. Paige's theory was that her picky friend was holding out for the ruler of the universe. She seriously doubted she would consider writing to Danny's friend unless he owned his own country.

Paige frowned at the pesky tax problem responsible for giving her a major headache and vowed upon Elvis' grave that she would never become a tax accountant no matter how enticing the salary might be.

She spied Danny's letter peeking out from under her book and her eyes widened. No way did she want her friend to see it. Tia was such a brat and, much as she pretended to be a cynic, she was a romantic at heart. So when she turned in her seat to greet another friend, Paige unobtrusively pulled the letter under the book.

"Not so fast! What are you trying to hide?" Tia wiggled her finger at her as she turned back to Paige. Before Paige could grab it off the table, Tia snatched it and turned the envelope over in her hands.

"APO address. Captain Daniel Napolitano. *Ooh!* You've got a soldier honey. You've been holding out on me, girlfriend." Unabashed, Tia extracted the letter and read it.

Heat scorched Paige's cheeks. She pretended nonchalance, and yawned behind her hand as if unconcerned that her friend was sticking her nose into her private affairs. "It's nothing. He's just a neighbor, my brother's best friend."

The twinkles didn't fade from Tia's eyes. She leaned forward on her elbows and spoke in a hushed, conspiratorial tone. "Is he cute?"

Paige's toes curled inside her clogs. Her fingers itched to pull the sunglasses resting on top of her head down over her eyes but that would be a dead giveaway. Besides, they were too light a tint of pink to hide her expression from such close range. "In a boy-next-door kind of way, I suppose. He's a total tease. He never let me forget I was one giant freckle when I was a kid."

Tia chuckled and clipped her hair at the nape of her neck with a long, sleek, pencil-thin barrette, casually elegant. "Did you ever go to bed with him?"

Shocked, Paige gaped at her friend hoping no one else had overheard. "I never!"

"With anybody? Or just not with him?" Mirth dancing in her eyes, Tia leaned forward eagerly and rested her chin on her hand.

What? Her best friend thought her a twenty-six-year-old virgin? "Just not with him. I've had lovers." A couple, not that even her closest friend needed to know such intimate details. "Just how many lovers have you had?"

"Simply scads. Just not lately." Tia's gaze scanned the letter, as if she found it extremely fascinating. "*Oh ho!* His friend wants to meet your friends. Why were you holding out on me?"

Surprised, Paige blinked. "I didn't think you'd be interested in a soldier, half a world away."

Tia pouted, folded the letter and passed it back to her. "Hey! I'm as patriotic as the next person. I do my part. I write to a couple of soldiers. I can handle one more."

The other woman's altruism was news to her. "Well, I was going to write to Danny today. Why don't you stick a letter to his friend in with mine?"

Tia's face glowed. "*Ooh!* I just adore soldiers. Especially officers." She whipped open her three-leaf binder, uncapped her lavender ink gel pen and began penning her note.

Paige watched in amazement at how easily Tia's words flowed to a total stranger. "What? You're giving him your complete autobiography?"

"Why not? The other guys I write to are starved for attention. They want to hear anything and everything, the more personal, the better." Tia squirted a dab of perfume on the page and then kissed it, leaving a scarlet imprint of her lips.

Scandalized, Paige stared at the paper. "You don't seriously want me to send this to him?"

"Sure, sweetie. The trick to being a great pen pal is to let your feelings pour forth. Make it fun. God knows our boys get little or none of that over there." The edge of Tia's mouth quirked and she winked. "The more open you are, the more open he'll be with you."

Paige gulped highly doubting she could be as *open* as Tia. "What if I pour out my soul to him and he laughs at me? This isn't some stranger I can fool into thinking I'm Princess Grace. He knows me. He saw me in braces and pigtails." She held out her arms as proof. "He knows I'm one gigantic freckle."

"Do you like him?" A strange glint lit her friend's eyes.

Paige veiled her glance with her stubby red lashes but knew she couldn't get away with lying to the other woman who knew her inside out. "Yeah."

"How much?" Tia's unrelenting stare made her jumpy.

"A lot...when he's not being a jerk."

"He sounded pretty sweet in that letter. This is your chance to seduce him. Don't blow it."

Paige bolted upright, her heart hammering against her ribs. "Seduce him? In a letter?" *God bless Tia. She was certifiable.* The men in the little white coats would appear any second to cart her away. If she went along with her, she'd be in the adjoining room at the sanitarium.

"Most definitely. It's a little underhand, but all's fair in love..." Tia shifted in her seat, her slim form graceful as a feline. A thoughtful expression flickered across her eyes. "He's single?"

"He's not married. I'm not sure if he's still dating with Penny..."

"Penny who?" Tia drummed her fingers on the table. "You've got to find out if she's still in the picture. But as long as he's not engaged or married, you still have a shot."

"His high school sweetheart. Head cheerleader. Senior Class President. Magnolia Queen." Paige wanted to gag on the other woman's resume. She'd never been any of those things, had never aspired to, but she still knew she couldn't compete with that kind of woman for a man who was obviously impressed by the gorgeous, popular types.

"Bummer. But it can still be done." Tia scrunched up her nose.

The students at the neighboring table scowled at them and a young man wearing horn-rimmed glasses hissed, "Hush!"

Undaunted, Tia frowned back at them. She packed up her books and stood. "Let's blow this joint and grab some grub. I'm starved. We can plan our strategy better at the Student Union anyway."

Paige stuffed her books in her backpack and hoisted it onto her shoulders, moaning inwardly. "Strategy?" Doom and damnation followed. Their stench made her stomach roil.

Her resolve to avoid all grease and carbs vanished the moment heavenly aromas hit her square in the face. "Give me a quarter-pound cheeseburger, fried okra and a double thick chocolate shake." She already hated herself but that wilted rabbit food was not about to touch her lips.

Tia tsk-tsked and shook her head. "What is that? The college diet?"

Bless her heart, Tia would have to stand up twice to cast a shadow. From a dieting standpoint, Paige's lunch was a nightmare. But her traitorous stomach rumbled, eager to devour it. Her spirits fell to her feet. "You know I have no willpower. I can't come here and nibble on salad while you're biting into a big juicy burger."

Tia paid for her meal and sashayed to a booth in the back, racking up several appreciative male gazes.

Paige trained her gaze directly ahead, not wishing to see derision on anyone's face concerning her heart attack on a plate. Ravenous despite the expensive diet pills, she was going to eat now and get back on her diet when she returned to the dorm.

Tia took out her new toy, a Palm handheld unit, and clicked her stylus on the mini screen. "You need major strategy if you're going to land an officer."

"I told you I'm not interested in hunting men." Tia made her sound so mercenary.

Tia just wrinkled her nose and tapped her stylus several more times. "First, you have to write very personal letters. I mean bare-your-soul, flirty letters."

"And second?" Paige groaned through a mouthful of beef. *Cyrano de Bergerac she wasn't.* She dabbed ketchup off her chin.

Tia pointed a finger at Paige's groceries. "You need to watch your intake. You've been saying that you want to drop weight for years. What are you doing about it?"

Paige stared cross-eyed at the enemy hamburger as it hovered midair between her plate and her mouth. Then with supreme effort, she wrestled it back to the dish. After wiping off her hands and her mouth, she shoved the food to the end of the table and hid it behind the menu.

She held up one finger. "Twice daily I take diet pills to curb my appetite. I've tried cutting out all carbs, eating only carbs, eating soup first at every meal, eating cereal for all my meals, eating cabbage soup 'til I was ready to sprout..." She could go on for hours. She'd tried just about every diet in existence...and failed miserably.

Tia rested her hand on her chin and tapped her fingers against her cheek. "If you were faithful, something should have worked."

Paige slid her gaze away. "I get so hungry..." *Starved was more like it.* "The only thing I haven't tried yet is surgery or hypnosis."

Tia grasped her hand. "Promise me you won't do that surgery. A friend of our family had it done and she's been deathly ill ever since."

"Actually, I was thinking about the hypnosis." If it weren't so expensive, she'd have done it by now. Maybe she could talk one of her friends into hypnotizing her. She eyed Tia speculatively. "Do you know how to hypnotize someone?"

Tia's jaw dropped open and she stared at Paige as if she'd lost her head. "You want *me* to hypnotize *you*?"

Paige nodded. "My business law professor was hypnotized to stop smoking almost two years ago and he's not lit up since."

"So what was stopping you from trying it?"

"Oh, just a little matter of money. It's only eight-hundred-dollars…" *At least.* She didn't earn that in an entire semester working part-time for pitiful student worker wages.

"Holy…"

"Exactly." The okra shouted to her and, if she didn't get out of here immediately, she was going to succumb. "Let's split."

"I'm going to take some pictures of you to send to that hottie and then it's letter-writing time." Tia's laughter tinkled over her. She tucked her arm through Paige's and dragged her back to the dorm.

"Photographs?" Paige panicked. She'd scare him to death and he'd have nothing else to do with her. "I'll break the camera. I won't fit on the film."

"Have a little faith, girlfriend. I'm pretty handy with a camera. With a little make-up and a few props, you'll wow his socks right off."

Paige eyed Dr. Frankenstein and tried to duck into a dark room. No one was going to capture her on film. And she defied anyone, even Tia or Merle Norman, to hide her infinite freckles.

"Don't you trust me?" Tia crossed her hands over her heart and hung her head.

Paige shuddered. "I never trust anyone who asks if I trust them."

Tia grabbed her arm and yanked hard, jerking her back into the hallway. "I promise it won't hurt a bit. I've got a digital cam at the apartment. If I have to, I'll do some graphic touch-ups."

"I hope you can do magic with that graphics program," Paige mumbled, a frisson of alarm creeping up her arm.

Tia lifted a strand of her stringy hair, echoing Paige's sentiments. "First, let's practice a little magic on that hair." Then she picked up Paige's hand and examined the nails. "Time to redo the manicure, too."

"Why not just a complete make-over?" Paige muttered sarcastically, feeling uglier than homemade soap.

"Excellent idea! Do you have any more classes today?" The merriment flashing in her friend's eyes did not bode well.

She wished she had a class, any class, as she couldn't take Tia's carryings-on. Even stats class would be preferable. "No. And I'm not scheduled to work, either."

* * * * *

"Dear Danny,

I've been dieting for a while now, so I didn't start it with you in mind...but I would like for you to see a slimmer me. Honestly? I'm ravenous. I asked my best friend Tia to hypnotize me to lose the urge to eat but she refused. She's afraid I'll start quacking like a duck or robbing banks. I'm so depressed. I've tried just about everything. Do you know how pathetic it is when you've worked out every day, cut out all carbs and STILL gain three pounds? I guess not, since you've lost fifteen pounds. Maybe I should join the army.

Tia's great. Most of the time anyway. She's the sister I never had. She's gorgeous, half Latin and half Polynesian. She's almost as big a tease as you. Well, at least as you used to be. Her letter for your friend is enclosed.

It's hard to imagine you on the other side of the world. What's it like there? Jackson is a big trip to me. Oh! We celebrated Mardis Gras in New Orleans last year. I went to the dog track in Mobile a couple months ago with some of the gals from my dorm.

You're very handsome in uniform. You must really get a workout over there. You have a lot more muscles.

Love,

Paige "

Tia hung over her shoulder as she signed her name to the letter.

"Do you mind? It's private." Paige tried to shield it with her body.

The other woman shook her head and picked up the letter. After reading it, she ripped it to shreds and let the pieces flutter to the floor. "You don't want to say that."

Paige whirled around in her chair, her claws bared. "Why not? What was wrong with it?"

"You want to seduce him, not put him to sleep." Tia perched on the side of the desk and yawned widely. "Do I need to dictate your letter?"

"No."

"Well, you need to be a lot more forward. And hip." Tia borrowed the pen and began writing. "You starred in my dreams last night. If you kiss half so well in real life, you'll turn my bones to butter…"

Paige's cheeks tingled. "I can't say that!"

Tia leaned close and stared into her eyes. "Sure you can. Just keep your eyes on the final goal. Remember, men love it when we think they're sexy. When we coddle them. When we ooh and ahh over their muscles and feats. That's the real secret to catching a man and any woman can do it, no matter what she looks like."

Tia's words held a convoluted logic. A man who could make her feel special, would be a real prize. But she feared such a man was as rare as a unicorn.

Tia smiled proudly at her and held out the pen to her as if she awarded a diploma. "Go get him, tiger." A wicked grin lit her face. "If you can't get in the mood, wear your sexiest, most scandalous lingerie while you write to him and imagine him ogling you."

Paige quivered with excitement and made a mental date with Frederick's of Hollywood. Cartoon character nightshirts had always been her speed but they couldn't be classified as remotely erotic, unless it counted how high they hitched up on her thunder thighs.

* * * * *

"Dear Danny,

I had the most erotic dream last night…and you starred in it. You were wearing your gun belt…and nothing else.

Tia gave me a trendy new 'do and we had a manicure and pedicure. I'm not the chipped-nail tomboy you remember. I'm obsessed with my nails now. I change the color and design at a minimum weekly. I love the fancy, decorative nails with rhinestones and glitter. Perfect to rake down a man's bare back…I just love to do that.

Tia snapped some pictures of me for you, which are enclosed. I bought some sexy new lingerie. Soon as I lose some weight, I'll send you a picture of me in it.

Tell me…do you have a big gun and grenades?

Love,

Paige"

Danny's internal furnace kicked up several degrees and he broke out in a sweat. *If Paige's letter didn't put pepper in the gumbo! This wasn't his first rodeo, but whew!* The steamy content singed his eyes.

Had she really said that or was he dreaming? Shell-shocked sounded more like it.

So Paige had dreamed about him. What did that mean? And she had dreamed about him being naked…and she had confessed it to him.

Was he copasetic with that? Hell yes. He hoped she dreamed he was royally fucking her, too. At least he could get some vicarious booty.

Frustrated he stared from her letter to the mysteriously seductive photos of herself in shadow, her face half-covered with floppy hats and big bouquets of roses.

His pulse raced. He'd never imagined himself naked, wearing only his gun. Her version of 'gun and grenades' obviously didn't equate to army standard issue and would never be used against the enemy. What he wouldn't give for a cold shower or a quick military transport to the base closest to the Delta.

He stared up at the shimmering moon nestled in a blanket of twinkling stars. Paige wouldn't see the same constellations from her vantage point in Hattiesburg but she'd see that same magical moon. Then he remembered the time difference. Dawn had broken in her part of the world and she'd be basking in the bright Gulf sunshine—if she had awakened yet.

He imagined her in bed, naked under her covers. Perhaps her dusky nipples peeked out from sexy, see-through lingerie. His mouth watered. He'd always wondered if freckles covered her entire body. Even over her breasts? Her promised land? He longed to connect the dots with his tongue, to kiss a hot trail from the tip of a pert nipple to her hot cunt. His cock grew hard and the ridge of his erection made his fatigues unbearably tight and uncomfortable. He cursed his vivid imagination and the heavy fatigues that gave no leeway. Of course if the army had wanted him to have a lady friend or an erection, they'd have issued them.

The next letter was from Rocco, who was recovering at a US army hospital in Germany. He chafed at being away from the action, being stuck in bed and having nothing to occupy his time except six-month old television re-runs. He had his eye on a hot little tiger-eyed nurse that gave awesome sponge baths. He couldn't wait for her to pounce on him.

So Danny had passed Paige's friend's letter onto Leo, his wingman now that Rocco had shipped out. The tall, lanky cowboy was starved for mail since his girl had dumped him.

By the time the unit had drilled all day and set up a new camp in case enemy intelligence had spotted their old one, his bones ached and he was hungry enough that even the military's ready to eat meal, the MRE, seemed tolerable. He had never enjoyed freeze-dried fruit. But hunger made a mighty fine sauce and he wolfed down the grub. Then he washed it down with warm lemonade wishing it was a tall glass of iced sweet tea, and played a game of pinochle with the guys until exhaustion claimed him.

He slept well for the first night in a long time, dreaming about erotic, freckled sirens in place of pestilence, death and bombs.

Paige sashayed across the desert sands, wearing her silky red hair fanned around her...and nothing else. As her hips swayed gently, her dusky nipples peeked out from beneath her silky tresses, making his mouth water and his cock stand at high alert. Bathed in desert moonlight, her creamy alabaster skin glowed. Freckles dusted her torso, all the way down to the red curls at the juncture of her thighs. He willed her closer so he could see if they dotted her mons.

A seductive smile curved her lips and her gaze never left his. Finally, she towered over him, an ethereal magnolia, and she licked her lips with the tip of her tongue. "May I join you in your sleeping bag, soldier?"

Tongue-tied, he opened it wide to her and patted the bag. He wished he could offer her a palace bed sprinkled with rose petals instead, but was willing to accept this gem anywhere, any time. Finally he found his voice. "Yes, ma'am."

He cursed his military bearing and tossed it into the desert sands. It had no place in bed with an exotic wildcat.

She stretched her long frame beside him, purring, her lips whisper-soft against his. "Can I see your *big gun*?"

He gulped and nodded, feasting his gaze upon her naked glory, mesmerized by the tight little buds of her nipples. Just as he'd imagined, freckles dusted her breasts so that he fancied her his spotted leopard princess.

She unsnapped his fatigues, unzipped him and released his full-blown erection into her hot hands. Her long, nimble fingers circled his girth, and then squeezed gently, eliciting a moan from deep inside him. "I love your *big gun*. Is it loaded?"

Oh yeah, and the safety was off. Where was his condom supply when he needed it? Magically, one popped into his hand and he ripped the foil package open with his teeth. A deep guttural growl rose from the depth of his loins and he pushed his pants off. He held the latex disc out to her. "Help me put this on."

She licked her lips again, glossy and enticing beneath dancing moonbeams. "Love to, sugar."

Exquisite torture rippled through him as her hands stroked his throbbing cock. He almost burst from her erotic ministrations, but held himself back with supreme effort. Finally it was in place and he couldn't wait another second. Dragging her to him, he rolled on top of her. They melded together perfectly. His cock nudged her squirming pussy, seeking her liquid heat. Much as he wanted to connect the dots, he couldn't wait to make her his.

"Love me." She must have read his mind. Her ample breasts rubbed against his chest in a purely primal mating dance. Her fingers curled around the base of his cock and stroked it against her swollen labia.

Not one to fall back and regroup, but to blaze full ahead, he thrust into her deeply. Her tight folds sheathed him. Her writhing intensified his pleasure to fever pitch. Her moans seeped into his bones. He drank deeply of her, their tongues mating wildly.

Gunpowder crackled deep in his core, igniting his nerve endings. Then his cannon exploded and he clasped her to him tightly.

A small creature writhed against his ankle and bit him, jerking him wide awake and causing the ethereal angel he had held in his arms only seconds before to evaporate into the midnight mist. Sudden, severe pain shot up his leg, making him jerk.

"What in hell?" Danny jumped out of his bag, the material entangling his feet, and he stumbled. The Iraqi desert was full of venomous creatures, several as deadly as enemy bullets. Only the week before, when crawling on his belly, he had come face–to–face with a full-hooded cobra.

He picked up his rifle, slipped the barrel inside the mouth of the bag and shook it out from a safe distance. A spiky, worm-like giant centipede fell to the ground, and then scampered under a nearby rock.

He didn't think it was lethal but it stung something terrible, and he fell to the ground, writhing in pain. "Man down. Need help," he said, panting, as the oxygen depleted from his lungs.

Leo's shaky form loped toward him and scooped him into his arms. "What happened, pardner?" Concern etched his craggy features and laced his voice.

"Insect bite…on my leg… down yonder." Danny tried to point to his ankle but the effort cost him and his head lolled back. "Centipede, I think." He hoped Leo understood his thicker-than-usual drawl. His tongue was so fat and his mouth was so dry he slurred his words. He couldn't remember if the creature was one of the poisonous varieties but he prayed not. Like Rocco, he didn't want to die on foreign soil, to be buried under shifting desert sands and lost to divine wrath like the Biblical city of Tanis. *Take him home and plant him in Dixie.*

Chapter Three

"Hey, Paige. Mind if I borrow your desk for a few?" Lucy, the campus internal auditor, swept into the campus computer store's back office where Paige was checking student credit reports.

"Sure thing. I've got a large stack of people to check so I'll be over here awhile." Paige typed in a new name and social security number and tapped her fingernails impatiently on the desk as she waited for the report to pop up on the screen. After this she still had to send out the hateful collection letters, a job she dreaded.

Lucy plucked a ledger off the shelf and sank her petite frame onto Paige's chair. "Everything going okay around here?"

If you didn't count her extreme boredom. "Just dandy." Paige jotted ratings down on the forms, and shook her head. This poor fellow didn't meet their loan qualifications. Feeling horrible, she placed his application on top of the mountain-high rejection stack. He'd be in one of the campus computer labs late at night.

"Who does the daily reconciliation?" Lucy stuck her glasses on her nose and peered at the book in front of her.

Alarm flooded Paige and her breath hitched in her throat. Everyone knew Lucy was the Saddam Hussein of auditors. "I'm one of the people. Arianna, Penny and Connor take turns. It just depends who's working at closing. Everything okay?"

Lucy smiled brightly up at her. "Yeah. Just doing the normal annual audit. Is there a schedule of when everyone works?" Lucy scooted the rolling chair back and grabbed a couple more of the ledgers and stacked them on the desk.

Stop being so paranoid! Auditors could smell fear, not that she was guilty of any wrongdoing. Paige pointed to the schedule pinned to the wall. "Paul keeps the current and next week's there. You'd have to ask him where he stores the old ones."

"Do you know when he'll be back?" Lucy's steady gaze made her squirm.

Paige glanced at the wall clock, praying that Paul would hurry up and rescue her. "Soon, I imagine. He probably just ran next door for a cola. Maybe Yolanda knows." A marketing grad student, Yolanda was their number one sales rep.

A shadow fell across the floor and Paul's rich baritone drifted to her. "Did I hear my name?"

"Just the man I need," Lucy said, standing and extending her hand. A small smile lit her unadorned face. "I need to sign these out for a couple of days and I need to see your old work schedules."

Paul frowned, his bottle poised at his lips. "Something wrong?"

Paige pretended to work, shuffling the credit applications as she listened intently. She jotted a couple of comments in pencil that could be erased later.

"Just a routine audit. Should I have my boss email your boss?" Butter dripped from the auditor's voice. *And vultures didn't prey on the weak.*

"That won't be necessary. Let me know how we can help. You have our full cooperation."

The words sounded innocent enough but Paige could tell from the way Paul bristled that it was a scary question.

"Fantastic. If I could take those now, I'll leave you to sell computers."

Paige forced herself to work in case Paul questioned her about anything. She couldn't leave until the letters were mailed out and she needed to study for her midterms.

An eternity later, Lucy packed her leather brief case and departed with a friendly wave.

Paul spoke close behind her without warning. "How are the apps going? Can we sell any computers today?"

She held up a small stack of promising reports to him. "These look good." She could practically hear the k'ching in his mind.

"Anybody home back there?" Penny Foster sailed in wearing a new power suit, Italian pumps and diamond stud earrings.

Somebody had a new sugar daddy. Paige couldn't afford to window shop at the boutiques that carried such uptown fashions, much less purchase them.

Paul's gaze lingered pointedly on the schedule. "Nice of you to join us."

Penny pouted prettily in her best wilted-magnolia impression. "My interviews at student employment ran late."

"It would've been nice if you'd warned us ahead of time." Paul crossed his arms over his chest.

"I thought I did. I'll put it in writing next time."

"Do that." Paul brightened as he scanned through the stack of promising credit applications.

When Paul had retreated to the main showroom, Penny rolled her eyes and poured a Café au lait into her mug. Steam curled up and she sipped gingerly, leaving lipstick imprinted on the rim. "It's only a silly student job. It's not like it pays enough to feed a hamster. It barely covers rent for family housing."

Paige had heard that family campus housing was dirt cheap, only a couple hundred dollars per semester. Of course, it was anything but luxurious, with cement block walls, and kitchens smaller than dog kennels. Red ants had been known to infest some of the apartments. So if Penny could just make rent with a child to support, how could she afford her new upscale outfit?

Paige swallowed her sigh, lamenting their miniscule pay. Still, the experience would build a good resume. "It's experience."

Penny flipped through a fashion magazine as if she had nothing better to do. "Ooh, isn't that precious?" She dog-eared a page depicting chenille tops and held it up for Paige to see.

Annoyed that Penny saw fit to loaf on the job, Paige counted to ten silently and reminded herself that Penny had helped her get this job, that she was a friend of Danny's. Of course, every time she reminded herself of that, she remembered how they had dated and that really raised Paige's ire toward the other woman, as unfair as it was. She schooled her features to hide her frustration. "Nice," she mumbled. It would be nicer if Penny would get up off her lazy butt and work.

"I haven't been able to get to the collection letters yet and it's three already." Paige made a concentrated effort to finish the current task. Her shift was due to end in half an hour, but only if those letters were mailed out.

Penny scrunched her nose and then picked up the phone and began speaking to a friend. She wedged the receiver between her ear and shoulder and painted her nails.

Typical…

"When you get off the phone, I could really use some help."

Penny frowned and put a hand over the phone receiver. In a hushed whisper, she said, "This is an important call. Can't you hold the fort?"

Important, her foot! When words like movies, television and food tripped off the woman's lips, she didn't think it was very important. Wasn't work important?

Obviously not, for Penny carried on the conversation for another good ten minutes while Paige chafed.

Ready to explode, Paige couldn't stay penned up in the back room with her. This was too much pressure for a minimum wage position, experience or not. The least she should be able to expect was that her co-workers pulled their weight so she didn't have to work like a field hand. This was the limit.

She sought out their boss. "I need a word with you in private." When Paul started walking to the back where Penny sat, she shook her head and pointed to a deserted corner of the store.

"What's up?" Paul tucked his thumbs into his pants pockets and perched on the edge of a desk.

"Penny's goofing off again. She's been on the phone since she arrived and I'm tired of doing all the work."

Paul frowned and sighed. "You know Penny's been telling me the same about you. I'm tired of the petty bickering."

Aghast at the blatant lie, Paige fumed. How dare Penny tell their boss false stories about her! "She's lying."

"How am I supposed to know whose lying? If I believed everything I was told, I'd have let you go long ago."

He didn't believe her. So he wasn't going to help? More bitterness welled up inside her.

"Word to the wise. Just do your job and learn to get along with your co-workers. Employers in the real world won't put up with this nonsense." Paul turned and walked away without another word.

Vexed, Paige marched back to her office and banged papers around her desk. Just as she finished stuffing the last envelope, Penny ambled out of the back room blowing on her nails.

Too furious to speak a civil word, Paige ran a damp sponge over the envelope and sealed it. Her pulse thudded, a sure indication her blood pressure was raising. Forcing a chipper note to her voice, she announced, "The letters are finished. I'm splitting."

"Paige, sugar. Would you please cover for me for just a couple more minutes more while I powder my nose and grab a drink?" Waltzing past regally, she didn't wait for Paige's response.

If that didn't curdle the milk. A scream strangled in Paige's throat as Penny's backside disappeared out the front door.

Paul stuck his head around the partition, his brows pinched. "Where's she going?"

To a job interview for another position, she hoped. Surely Paul didn't want the truth after his lecture about bickering. She swallowed a sharp retort and replaced it with a bland, "Powder room."

"Okay." He disappeared, mumbling under his breath.

Penny straggled back about an hour and a half later at closing time, as Paige ran the closing reports. "I ran into an old friend I haven't seen in simply ages. I hope you don't mind I was a tad delayed."

Steamed, Paige was of a mind to go over Paul's head and file a formal complaint with his boss. "If this job interferes in your social life so much, you should consider giving it to someone who wants it and needs it. I've missed my study group."

Shock flitted across Penny's hazel eyes and her hand fluttered to her throat, the epitome of Southern belle-dom. "I desperately need this job so I can support my baby. With all due respect, you should have let me know if I was being such a huge imposition."

Paige was ill that she had ignored decorum to such an extent. Why didn't the other woman work harder to protect her job if it was so extremely important? Graduate student or not, Penny didn't have a lick of sense. How could Danny have dated her?

Still, Paige's heart went out to the innocent child, so she bit her tongue.

* * * * *

"Road trip. The Alpha Psi Kappas are going to the French Quarter. Come with?" Tia donned a Mardis Gras mask and dusted a long feather across Paige's neck, making her shiver.

Tempting as a Pat O'Brien Hurricane and sultry jazz sounded, she couldn't. *A quiet weekend when everyone else was down in New Orleans sounded like the perfect time to get to study in quiet.* "Can't this time. This term paper's due." Paige shrugged apologetically as she surfed the net for more info on her thesis.

Tia faced off against her and anchored her hands on her hips. "When?"

Paige tilted her head and squinted up at Ms. Pushy. "In two weeks."

Tia stole the mouse and clicked off Internet Explorer. "You're officially kidnapped. Put on your prettiest party dress and dancing shoes." She crooked her finger at Paige and then pointed forcefully at the closet.

It drove her crazy waiting 'til the last minute to complete assignments. "But…"

"I know all the naughty lingerie shops in the Quarter," Tia said in a singsong voice. "Remember your soldier honey…"

Paige grimaced recalling the dismal state of her checking account, starting to wish she could join the girls. She loved the French Quarter. Jimmy had been conceived there during her parents' honeymoon so it held special romantic sentiments for her. But she was a steel magnolia, so she held strong. "I really can't. I'm broke."

"Consider it an early birthday present. I'd never forgive myself if I allow you to let an officer and a gentleman wriggle off your hook."

An absurd vision of Danny naked, his cock long and throbbing for her as he dangled on a fishing hook, teased her. She bit back a ribald giggle.

"Shake it. A Hurricane with my name is calling to me."

Three hours later, Paige was gasping in shock in the back room of a French lingerie shop. "You want me to wear *that*?" Paige pointed to the bustier the petite sales woman modeled. "No way can my ten-gallon bosom fit in that bit of fluff." *She'd pass out if her ribs didn't snap first.*

"I think something a little…softer would be better," Tia said echoing her thoughts. Thoughtfully, she tapped her chin with her forefinger.

The model pirouetted on her spiky fur high heels and returned shortly in a sheer full circle skirted lavender baby doll with yards of delicious gathered lace trim. The woman didn't blink an eyelash that her very admirable attributes were clearly revealed in the scandalous gown.

No way could she wear that. She'd frighten herself every time she passed a reflective surface.

Instead, Paige favored the more demure baby doll trimmed with lace, ruffles and satin ribbons. One with a scalloped red lace flounce was adorable. The G-string made her pause but at least the full skirt would provide some cover. That would light her fire and free her inner sex demon when she wrote to Danny.

"We'll take the last two you showed us." Tia held out her credit card to the beaming saleswoman.

The woman eyed Tia's trim figure appreciatively. "Petite for you, madame?"

"They're for my friend." Tia indicated Paige and the woman winked at her suggestively.

"Oui, madame. We carry Goddess sizes. Let me point out the pièce de résistance." Unabashedly, she untied the ribbon over her bodice and her rosy nipple burst out.

Goddess, huh? That was one way to put it.

Highly uncomfortable, Paige blinked and averted her eyes. *Only in the Quarter.* As they departed the shop, Paige hissed, "I didn't say I liked those."

"And prude you are, you never would. But I saw the expression on your face. It's you. Happy birthday." Tia kissed her cheek and held out the bag to her.

"I need that Hurricane now." Otherwise she'd never get the nerve up to wear either piece of lingerie, even in private. But she accepted the package and held it securely.

"You're on. I'm parched." Not one to dally, Tia wended her way down the flagstoned Bourbon Street to St. Peter's Street. She navigated through droves of milling tourists, mimes and other colorful street performers. Jasmine and magnolia fragranced the air, vying with the luscious scents of frying beignets, simmering seafood gumbos and fresh baked French rolls, which made her stomach rumble unbearably.

Paige shuddered, wishing she'd stayed safely home away from this dieter's Devil's Triangle, despite the splendor of lushly serene hidden courtyards that peeked through wrought iron gates.

That night, or rather the next morning, when they dragged back into Hattiesburg, she found a note from her roommate, Merline, pinned to her pillow. *"I won't be back 'til late Sunday. Just let my phone take messages 'til I return. You're a doll."*

Still wide-awake, reveling in her rare aloneness, she slipped on her decadent peek-a-boo baby doll and turned down her bed coverlet. She lit several scented candles and turned soft jazz on the stereo, letting it crawl inside and capture her heart with its seductive romantic passion.

Then she propped herself up on her pillows and wished Danny lay beside her instead of bedding down on desert sands half a world away.

"Dear Danny,

Tia and Alpha Psi whisked me away to New Orleans last night where I bought some very naughty lingerie--black lace trimmed with ruffles and satin ribbons with a G-string and a very sheer lavender baby doll. Then we imbibed Hurricanes from Pat O'Brien's and partook of beignets and po' boys. We danced in the street 'til we couldn't take another step. And then we piled into horse drawn carriages and let them cart us back to our cars. How magical it would be to make languorous love in the back of a horse-drawn carriage. Did you know that Jimmy was conceived in one? It's my deepest, darkest fantasy, too.

Okay...that was a lie. My very deepest, most dearly held fantasy is to be handcuffed to a bed. I will be totally submissive to my lover and he will make me squirm and writhe with unimaginable delights."

Squirming, she imagined being handcuffed to a king-sized bed, her legs spread wide and her pussy naked and vulnerable to Danny's every whim. Her hand skimmed her breasts, and traveled down her belly to her clit. She stroked it, pleasuring herself. Closing her eyes, she dreamed Danny licked her pussy and massaged her clit.

"I can't believe I just divulged my most fervent sexual fantasy to my older brother's best friend. Blasted Hurricanes!"

She giggled and her gaze drifted to her souvenir Hurricane glass adorning her desk. The delightfully potent drink had slid down her throat and erased her inhibitions. It was a good thing she didn't get to Louisiana much.

"I'm absolutely, positively, completely livid at myself for inhaling all that food. Of course, who can visit New Orleans and

not partake of their culinary delights? They'd have to be stronger souls than me. But I'm not going to shed pounds consuming such rich food. I'm cursed. All I have to do is look at food – think of food – and the pounds multiply. I have absolutely no willpower. Zip. Zilch. Nada. I so long to be slim and beautiful by the time you come home but it's a lost cause. When I was good and stuck to my diet, I still gained weight. I'm cursed. Cursed."

She frowned at her soft, Rubenesque body, bulging in all the wrong places. One of her enemies must have fashioned a voodoo doll of her that prevented her from shaping up. Probably Penny...

Having lost the mood, she scribbled her name and enclosed the letter in an envelope. Not wanting Merline to find it if she snooped about, she slipped into her heavy chenille robe and slippers and padded outside to the mailbox where she posted this too-hot-to-hold baby before she lost her nerve.

Chapter Four

Danny's jaw dropped wide when he read Paige's latest missive. She wanted to be handcuffed to the bed and be submissive? To him?

He longed to help her out, both with her fantasy and losing weight. Visions of the redhead tied to a large bed, nude, totally at his mercy, made his cock stand embarrassingly at attention. He would be the master and run the show. Why stop at fur-lined handcuffs and chains? Why not nipple clamps? He could really pleasure her with a few other sex toys, too. *Feathers. Whips...*

He would blindfold her to keep her guessing and, when she was very, very good, he would reward her. And when she wasn't, he would spank her.

"Dear Paige,

It's a nightmare of daily attacks, death and vicious sandstorms. Dust still lingers in the air even though last night's storm has abated. The fighting seems worse since the president officially proclaimed major combat operations ended. There's talk that we won't be rotated out like planned, that our battalion may have to remain a year or more. The numbers of terrorists have multiplied like cockroaches. Some say this is Vietnam all over. I pray not, but it sure seems like it here."

He wouldn't dare alarm her with talk of almost daily suicide car bombings, supposed civilians ambushing them, guerillas shooting rocket propelled grenades and using improvised explosive devices against the occupation forces. He certainly wouldn't tell her of his recent brush with the poisonous insect that had laid him up for several days. Nor would he tell her that his platoon seemed to be in the epicenter of resistance.

"Perhaps I shouldn't have told you this as I know how you worry. Believe me, I've not told you half and I'm not going to. But I need someone to confide in and you're my lifeline to home and the real world. Your letters lift me out of this hellhole and give me something to look forward to. Don't stop writing to me. I anxiously await each new day now instead of dreading it, because I get to talk to you, to share your joy and your dreams.

Sometimes I wonder why God has spared my life? What does he have in store for me?

Any chance I can get pictures of you in your hot new lingerie??? ALL of you? Ooh baby! I'm hot just thinking about you in your see-through nighties.

If I were home, I'd help you exercise."

He grew hot thinking about precisely how he would help her work out and it wasn't jogging outside. Some major bed Olympics would be in order. And a master's tournament of connect the dots.

"I'll make you a deal. I'll owe you a kiss for every pound you lose. No cheating. Start keeping tally so you don't forget how many kisses I owe you. You'll collect when I get home. Soldier's honor."

He swiped the perspiration from his forehead sure it wasn't generated from the oppressive desert heat. How he wanted to drink deeply of her lips and taste her sweet ambrosia. How he wanted to feel the soft pillows of her breasts molded against his chest, feel her warmth seep into his cold bones.

Artillery barrage rumbled across the desert, shattering his pleasant reverie. Banshee sirens wailed and he swore under his breath. Nearby Arabic voices chilled him. He dropped the letter, dressed in his gas mask and grabbed the assault rifle lying by his feet. Then he stuffed the letter into his pocket as he joined up with Charlie Company.

Muzzled flashes lit the night sky. More sirens cried across the city. Then a large plume of gray smoke swirled into the sky, eclipsing his view of the moon. His Major shouted orders and gunfire exploded so he dove to the ground as several bullets whizzed by his head.

"The Major's down!" Leo shouted, raw agony in his voice. The lanky second lieutenant lay prostrate beside the fallen man, taking his pulse.

As second in command, Danny gritted his teeth and took charge. "Get him to the medics. Everyone else advance."

Why were they were still fighting a war that had supposedly been won? Yet more men and women had died during the occupation than the war. If this wasn't war, what was it?

* * * * *

"BAGHDAD, 20 October — A suicide car bomb attack on cleric headquarters claimed at least ten lives. Five US soldiers and at least five civilians died as a result of the explosion. Residents said a firefight broke out upon US forces following the bombing. The violence heightened tensions between the American occupation force and Iraqis in a country already plagued with almost daily attacks against US troops more than a year after the official cease of hostilities."

Paige's gut clenched. The newsprint slid out of her fingers, onto her desk. Danny could be one of the injured…or dead. She bowed her head on the desk.

Would anyone notify her? Should she call his family for information? She didn't want to worry them unnecessarily or add to their grief. Would Jimmy know? And if he did, would he think to tell her? She didn't think her brother was aware of the new dimension to her relationship with his best friend and she wasn't sure how he would take it if he knew.

A finger poked her on the shoulder and her heart dove to her knees. Whirling around, her hand went to her throat.

Tia stepped back, worry creasing her brow. "Are you okay?"

Silently, Paige handed the paper, folded to the article, to her friend. She waited impatiently while her friend scanned the news, her nerves jumping, her mind casting a thousand gloomy scenarios. She grabbed a chocolate bar out of her top desk drawer, desperately in need of comfort, and took a big bite.

"He told me it was still bad over there but I didn't realize it was still a war zone." What alternate universe had she been sleeping in? "I can't believe I said those things to him in my last letter." Paige moaned, slapping the desktop with the flat of her hand, making invoices float to the carpet.

"What things?" Tia leaned against the empty desk, balanced her art portfolio against the wall and then crossed her ankles, making her silver plated ankle bracelet jingle.

Paige crouched down and gathered the documents into a semi-neat pile and struggled to stand back up. "How could I have gone on about such trivialities when men are dying?" When Danny was wondering if each second was his last? When he faced enemy gunfire and assault?

"What trivialities?" Tia crossed her arms over her chest and gazed at her with a mixture of concern and curiosity.

Paige glanced around, making sure the boss and her coworkers weren't eavesdropping. "Remember the night we got a little tipsy in N'awlins on those Hurricanes? And bought that naughty lingerie?"

Tia cracked a grin. "Barely. The part after the Hurricanes is still really fuzzy. I didn't do anything too embarrassing, did I? And if I did, was he cute?"

Paige grimaced and massaged her aching neck. "You didn't. But I did." When her friend's eyes widened, she continued, "I tried on some of that sexy lingerie you gave me for my birthday, like you suggested, and I wrote to Danny." She licked her dry-as-sand lips. "I told him all about the lingerie, how I'd like him to see it, and that my deepest, darkest fantasy is to be handcuffed to the bed…naked…and submissive."

Tia clapped her hands sharply and smiled. "Yes! That's a good thing." She beamed on Paige like she would a star pupil.

Paige snatched the report back for the scrapbook she was going to start. "Not if he's dead."

Tia sobered and pushed off the wall. She crossed to Paige and laid a comforting hand on her shoulder. "There are thousands of troops over there. Until someone calls you with bad news, don't borrow trouble."

"That's easy to say when you're not emotionally involved…"

"Stop it. Worrying won't help him. And I have struck up friendships with some of the men, remember." She lowered her voice to a whisper. "Especially your friend's buddy, Leo…"

And the chances were equal that Leo could be a casualty. Or both men… Paige breathed in deeply and rolled her shoulders to work out the kinks. "I'll try to stay strong."

"When do you get sprung? Have you checked your mail yet?"

Paige's gaze sought out the clock on the wall. "Penny was supposed to be here ten minutes ago but it's anyone's guess when she'll show up."

"Like that, is it?" Tia pursed her lips. Her gaze traveled to the student post office across the hall. "If you trust me with your key I'll check your box and be right back."

She trusted her friend with her life so she dug her keys out of her pocket and dropped them into Tia's outstretched palm. The box number was imprinted on the key so she didn't bother to repeat it for Tia's benefit. She could read. "Thanks. I've not heard from him in a couple weeks. That has me worried, too."

"Leo mentioned he'd been bitten by some scorpion or centipede…" Tia's eyes grew wide and her hand flew to her mouth. "I wasn't supposed to mention that."

A deadly scorpion? Alarm flooded her and she grasped her friend's wrist. "Is he okay?"

"He got lucky. It only bit him once. Twice could have been fatal." Tia readjusted her hair, reclipping it in her low, stylish ponytail. "At least that's what Leo told me."

Paige moved to the backroom and signed onto the Internet. "Do you remember exactly what bit him?" She typed 'deadly insects Iraq' into the search engine and tapped her fingers on the keys impatiently awaiting the results.

"Some kind of centipede, I think. Leo didn't fill me in on all the details." Tia backed away, the key dangling from her fingers. "I'll be back in a few."

Paige fluttered her fingers over her shoulder, her attention focused on her research. To her horror, it seemed the soldiers faced more deadly enemies than just the human variety. Venomous snakes and insects abounded in the desert sands of Iraq.

"Mail call!" Tia skipped in happily, holding out an airmail envelope.

Her heart pounding against her ribs so hard they were in danger of breaking, Paige snatched her mail from the other woman's fingers. She inhaled deeply before tearing into it. The postmark was prior to the date of the bombing, so that didn't prove Danny was safe.

She scanned the letter quickly for any mention of the insect bite or illness, but found none. Then she reread it slowly, savoring his words, letting his essence seep into her. Heat suffused her chest and crawled up her neck and into her cheeks. She gasped and blinked when she read the part about earning a kiss for every pound she lost, unable to believe her eyes.

She blinked again and stared at the words until they blurred. The tease couldn't really mean it? At least no more seriously than she'd been about being tied up in bed at a man's mercy. She'd been drunk out of her skull when she'd written that. She'd have never said that sober. Did he have the excuse that he was drunk? Neither liquor nor alcohol was alluded to in the letter.

Chocolate? Or Danny's intoxicating kisses? No contest! Shivering, she dropped the candy bar on which she had been nibbling. Even if he was just flirting and all she could expect from this game was his imaginary kisses, she couldn't pass them up. The chocolate completely lost its allure.

Tia rushed to her side, startling her. She'd forgotten her friend was in the room she'd been so engrossed in Danny's letter. "What's wrong? Is Leo okay? Is Danny all right?"

Paige couldn't push words past her lips. They stuck in her throat. So she held the letter up to her friend.

Tia's jaw dropped open wide and then she mumbled, "*Mama mia.*" She confiscated the partially consumed chocolate bar and tossed it in the trash. Shaking a finger at Paige, she said, "No more."

Penny breezed in, her hair newly frosted, her nails freshly manicured and new shoes donning her feet. She stopped dead, her gaze ping-ponging from one friend to the other. "What did Paige do this time?"

Paige sent a silent plea to Tia not to divulge any information about Danny's letter. "I didn't do anything." She batted her lashes at her coworker, anxious to escape. "Nothing to report. Tia and I have to scoot. See you later."

"Wait! I'm not clocked in yet. I need to use the ladies' room."

Paige checked her watch, scowling when she saw that Penny was twenty minutes late already. "We're late. See if Yolanda can cover for you."

"Late for where?" Tia hissed in Paige's ear.

"Anywhere," Paige whispered, corralling her friend through the throng of humanity, out into the bright afternoon sunshine.

"You should call and speak to him. That would alleviate your mind."

"We can? I don't have a phone number for him." Paige nibbled her bottom lip. "But maybe his family does." If she played it cool, she could tell them she was thinking about Danny and just wanted to know if friends could call and send their well wishes.

"Leo told me about this Operation Phone Home thing and I checked it out on the web. We can send them a calling card so they can call us."

Paige punched her friend in the arm. "And you didn't tell me?"

"Ouch!" Tia put a few steps between them as she rubbed her arm. "I just got the letter this morning. You've been working."

"Okay, you're forgiven."

"I wonder if they have email?" Tia looked dreamily into the distance.

"Just general message boards for congratulating the troops. At least that's all their platoon has access to." She wished they had email or, better yet, instant messaging. Warm tendrils of desire coursed through her at the thought of talking to Danny daily. She'd be getting herself in even more trouble than she was now.

A strong disco beat flooded the dorm hallway when they entered the building. "The seventies won't die," Paige mumbled, frowning. Her neighbor Amy played the infernal music all day and all night 'til she wanted to scream.

Her room wasn't much better. Not only could she hear Amy's disco through the paper-thin walls, but Merline's soaps blared in the room, trying to drown out the disco.

Tia pulled her aside. "How do you ever get any work done here?"

She grimaced. "This is why God invented libraries." She'd rather study in the comfort of her pajamas, using her own computer, but dorms weren't conducive to such pleasantries. At least not this one.

"Grab your stuff and we'll go to my apartment." Tia banged on the wall. "Give it a break! Disco's dead!"

When hip-hop broke the sound barrier and started shaking the far wall, Paige moaned. "I wish I could afford my own apartment." But she was blessed with this scholarship so she shouldn't complain. It would be impossible to work a full-time job with graduate school. It was hard enough working part-time on campus with flexible hours that were friendly to her classes.

They dodged moss fluttering in the slight breeze and picked their way through pecans scattered across the broken sidewalk as they made their way to Tia's bungalow just off campus. Honeysuckle tickled Paige's nostrils and she sniffed appreciatively. It was so much more laid back here than Fraternity Row, just a few blocks away. This antebellum world soothed her frazzled nerves, although she was still anxious to call Danny's mother and get his information.

She kicked off her shoes and settled in on her friend's daybed, letting the soft strains of Tia's favorite Mozart wrap her in its warmth. After calling information and getting Danny's parents' number, she dialed them and spoke to Miss Evelyn, his mother.

"Danny would love to hear from his friends. He gets so lonely and I'm such a horrible correspondent, with my carpal tunnel." Miss Evelyn rambled on.

Tia nudged her and whispered, "Find out what kind of goodies he likes and his underwear size."

Scandalized, her gut clenching, Paige gaped up at her friend. Covering the receiver with her hand, she hissed, "I'm not asking Miss Evelyn what his underwear size is."

"All the guys desperately need it. Don't be shy." Tia grabbed for the phone as if she would ask the question.

Paige turned away and mustered her courage. She clenched the phone tighter in her fingers. "Does Danny need anything? My friend and I are putting together a care package. Clothing? Favorite foods? Favorite games?"

Tia winked at her and poised her pen over a notepad, stenographer-style. "Very sly. Don't forget to get his size."

Clearing her throat and closing her eyes, she asked, "What sizes does he wear?"

Aloud, she repeated Miss Evelyn's suggestions and advice while Tia took dictation.

"He absolutely adores red licorice. And he likes boxers, so he has plenty of room to move around."

Paige's furnace almost boiled over as she croaked, "He prefers boxers."

Tia grinned and said, *soto voce*, "So he needs lots of room. He just gets better and better. An officer, a gentleman and a really big …"

Paige hurled a decorative pillow at her friend to shut her up before she was too embarrassed to live. Nor did she want Tia's grubby little mind dreaming about Danny's big anything. She had him and his cock staked out. Tia would just have to dream about Danny's friend, Leo, or one of her other soldiers.

Finally, an eternity later, Paige bid Danny's mother goodbye with a promise to visit at Christmas.

Tia bounded off the bed and slung her purse over her shoulder. "Let's go shopping. We have to send them a huge care package."

Paige mourned the sorry state of her checkbook. "I'm a pauper. They only pay us student worker peons once a month."

Tia sagged onto her deep chair. "I'm not very flush, either." She tapped her finger against her lip.

Paige noodled the problem and then brightened when an idea came to her. "Maybe we can sponsor a fundraiser, get some other students to support the troops. If everybody gives a little, it won't be too hard on anyone. And we can send enough for Danny's platoon."

Tia perked up and snapped her fingers. "The Alpha Psis will help! They're always looking for a good cause."

Tia took Paige before the high council of the Alpha Psis. The president, Neresa Culpepper, was a graduate drama major., The vice president, Melanie Jo Boudreaux, was a senior marketing major. Both young women seemed eager to enlist in the cause.

"The Psis would love to help our boys overseas. It's the least we can do," Neresa said, tapping the end of her pencil on the sloppy desk. "But we need to know food preferences and clothing sizes. And we have to set up some fund raisers."

Melanie Jo became animated, excitement radiating in her bluish-violet eyes. "Like car washes. Or a crawfish boil. Maybe sell yellow ribbon pins."

Tia nudged Paige's knee with her own and sent her an excited I-told-you-so glance.

Neresa pursed her mauve glossed lips. "I've heard that general care packages are being refused for security purposes. So we'd need names and addresses of individual soldiers, I reckon. We'd have to set up pen pals between your boyfriends' friends and the Psis." She leaned heavily on her elbows and stared into Paige's eyes. "Can you match up our Psis with the soldiers, one-on-one? I'm sure our ladies would be most amenable."

Paige gulped at the magnitude this project was taking, simultaneously ecstatic but shaking in her shoes.

Tia, wide-eyed and trembling herself, stuck her hand across the desk and shook both women's hands. "Deal. We'll get the names ASAP. And pictures of the men."

"We need a name for this project to submit to our membership and National. What do you call it?"

Paige's mind went blank save for "underwear" and she wouldn't saddle such a noble cause with an uninspired and embarrassing tag like "Operation Underwear". So she went slack-jaw and stared at her friend like an idiot, hoping for divine inspiration.

A pensive gleam pushed the joy from Melanie Jo's eyes. "What about 'Save Our Soldiers'. 'SOS' for short or 'Operation PenPal'?"

Tia cracked a grin. "It has flair. I like it." She held up her hands and mimed 'SOS, Save Our Soldiers'."

"How about '*Serve* Our Soldiers'?" Underwear and red licorice wouldn't exactly save their men-at-arms. Plus she didn't want to jinx them and she could take a solid pride in it.

Neresa rose with a southern belle's grace, beaming at them. "We'll start arranging the fund raisers and you set us up with pen pals and lists of what they can use. The city of Meridian has a website that lists a lot of good items to include in care packages if you need ideas."

Paige glanced about the palatial parlor set on the third story of the Alpha Psi sanctuary. She asked, "About how many members will be wanting pen pals, do you reckon?"

Melanie Jo scrunched her pert nose. "We have about one hundred active magnolias in the Delta chapter."

One hundred? Paige gulped and her heart thudded heavily against her ribs. She didn't think Danny's platoon had even half that many men. And she didn't know if he even had close enough contact with other platoons to arrange for more soldiers to participate. And, if so, did he have to get permission?

When she opened her mouth to express her concern, Tia squeezed her fingers hard and shook her head, as if reading her thoughts. She clamped her lips tightly.

Tia clapped her hands and then rounded the desk to hug her friends and kiss their cheeks. "We'll get you those names right away. Let us know how we can help with the fund raisers."

Melanie Jo chuckled. "Don't worry. We will. I'm going to get right on it and order those pins, and set up a crab boil."

Paige's stomach rumbled. She could practically taste the scrumptious seafood. That reminded her she hadn't eaten so much as a morsel of food in hours and the cafeteria wouldn't be open much longer. Of course the fast food joints off campus stayed open late but she needed to conserve her meager funds to help Danny. She exchanged the obligatory hugs and kisses and made her departure.

The gyros and tacos smelled heavenly, beckoning her to assuage her hunger, but Danny's letter burned against her thigh, reminding her of his promised rewards for her diligence. *No*, she grimaced. Only for her success. He would demand proof of her diligence in the form of lost weight and inches. And Tia had appointed herself official weekly weigher so she couldn't fib. Sometimes, like in this instance, her friend was a royal pain.

So she passed by the delicious aromas and made a salad out of a mixture of lettuces, sliced radishes, green onions and sliced carrots. The cheese and croutons tempted her unmercifully but she envisioned slow, languorous kisses from Dan instead.

At first, the kisses were chaste, on her lips, but that wasn't sufficient ammunition against her ravenous hunger pangs. His kisses grew more ravenous and he drank of her deeply, making her knees weak and her breathing shallow. Then he trailed his fiery lips around her arched jaw and nibbled on her ear lobes as his hands caressed her back. His tongue dipped into her ear canal, making her tremble. He stroked her hair back and nibbled her ear as he settled her on his lap against his very obvious, throbbing erection, which threatened to burst out of his fatigues, and now teased her belly.

She writhed against him, moaning her pleasure. In a husky, breathless voice, she murmured, "Kiss my nipples."

He growled and ripped her blouse open, the buttons popping, flinging across the room. A tiger now, he pushed her shirt and then her bra off, freeing her heavy breasts to his voracious, heated gaze.

He dropped angel kisses to each pebbling nipple in turn, setting off a chain of explosions in her.

Wonderful as his soft lips had felt, she was greedy for more. "Haven't I earned more kisses than that?"

Breathing heavily, his eyes filled with raw hunger and he shook his head slowly, almost regretfully. "No, sugar. The bank's empty. You have to earn more kisses."

Burning up, longing for him to suckle her breasts and then kiss her pussy, she tried to seduce him by rubbing her nipple across his lips. "Can't you extend me a little..." She rubbed against his hot erection and licked her lips suggestively, "...credit? I swear I'll pay it back." She'd give him the most fantastic blowjob a man had ever or would ever know. She would handcuff him to the bed and then take his big cock as far into her mouth as it would go. She would lick it, savor it and milk it until he came long and hard inside her. His sweet seed would be creamy and she would become addicted to it. Then her aching, greedy pussy would demand its turn and she'd straddle him, hovering just above the tip of his gloriously swollen dick, teasing him until she couldn't stand to be another second without him inside her. But she wouldn't glove him immediately. She would give him an inch at a time, then pull up, and keep doing that until he was so hot for her cunt that his hips arched off the bed and thrust into her hungrily.

But he wouldn't have her quite yet. She would pull off and roll on the latex protection she had nearly forgotten in her frenzy to ride his cock.

By now, she'd be so hot for him, so glazed with passion, she'd forget playing games and slide all the way down on him, filling her with his swollen shaft. She would ride him like a bronco, squeezing his cock tightly in her folds, and let rapture overcome them.

By the time she uncuffed him, he'd forget all about her balance sheet, credit and everything else except possessing her, that he would screw her all night without mercy until they ran out of all the boxes of condoms she had stockpiled.

Slowly, she awoke from her stupor and found herself sucking on a carrot stick in a back, corner booth. Her fantasies were getting out of hand and she hoped she hadn't made a fool of herself.

She downed her tasteless salad and escaped the torturous odors, her stomach protesting. She dropped her purse off at the dorm, changed into jogging clothes and took a sunset jaunt around the campus, hoping the exercise would quell her appetite. While she was listening to her portable radio, an ad for weight loss by acupuncture caught her attention. She cursed the fact she didn't have a pen and paper handy to write down the contact information so made a mental note to look for it on the Internet when she returned to the dorm.

But fragrant honeysuckle and the gorgeous twilight seduced her into a longer jog than planned and exhausted, she fell onto her bed.

Chapter Five

"You got the Forbes report there, buddy?" Leo hunkered down beside Danny and stretched out his long, bowed legs. He opened his own letter from home and let out a whoop and a holler.

Danny drank in Paige's words as he fingered the calling card she had enclosed. She wanted to talk to him, hear his voice. And she wanted to send a care package to him. More over, she wanted his comrades' names so her friends could send specialized packages to them, too.

"Ooh, doggie! Tia wants to send us some care packages. And she needs my dimensions." Leo shuffled his large frame uncomfortably. "She wants me to make out a wish list. I wonder if she can fit herself in there, too."

Fear and excitement battled for supremacy inside Danny, making his heart flutter. What had begun as a harmless friendship had morphed into a little flirtation, and now seemed to be taking on tremendous proportions.

He accepted the blame for stoking the heat to higher, more dangerous levels, but he had figured she was just having a little fun, like him.

But somewhere in the midst of their correspondence, true feelings had blossomed and she'd become his lifeline. He lived for her letters, for her flirty words and glimpses into her mind and soul. If not for the war, much as he hated it and being stuck in this sandy hell, he never would have been afforded this opportunity to truly know her.

This gem had lived next door to him about forever and he'd been blind to her brilliance.

Now that he could see it, he feared he was spoiled for any other. *No.* What he feared was that she didn't return his growing feelings and that she was just doing her patriotic duty to support the troops and he was her pet project.

Her words scorched the corneas of his eyes. He devoured her latest letter. Her letters arrived almost daily now, sometimes even twice daily. His cock grew rock-hard.

"Dear Danny,

I called your mother today to find out your favorite food and your clothing sizes. Before I buy anything, I want to double-check with you as you had told me you've lost weight.

Tia and I are holding fund raisers with the Alpha Psis but, as we can't send general care packages anymore, nor can we send one or two giant ones to you and Leo, the Alpha Psi's want to become pen pals with your friends. Do you have one hundred friends who don't get mail and would like to? Please send their names and addresses right away and we'll match them up.

I dream about your kisses. They're inspiring me to lose weight but, I fear, to be naughty, too. I may have embarrassed myself in the cafeteria last evening when I envisioned you kissing me. I don't remember how I got from the salad bar to the booth, only that, the next thing I knew, I was sucking on a big, fat carrot."

Whew! His cock flexed, tenting his fatigues. He wished she were sucking on it now. Again, he tried to caution himself that she might not mean what it sounded like. Or if she meant it to sound as it did, that she might just be a consummate flirt. Well, if she was, two could play that game and he could make her as hot for him as she was making him for her. By the time he went home, she'd be begging to suck his cock for real. He made up his mind to start an all-out campaign to win her heart, soul and body. Whether she knew it or not, the siege had begun.

He laid his plans in motion using the phone card she sent to him, staying up 'til the early a.m. to catch her early evening, Mississippi time.

Tia tells Leo you're taking diet pills. Stop that! You might as well come here and walk into the middle of a minefield. I don't want anything to happen to you. He came dangerously close to adding, I need you, but wasn't ready to reveal his entire heart. It scared him how important she was becoming to him.

Homesickness assailed him, not only for Paige but also for Biloxi. He missed the smell of shrimp and seaweed wafting in from shore. He missed the sound of the ocean. He missed crabbing on full moonlit nights while shrimp boats bobbed on the horizon.

When I get back, I want to take you to Biloxi Beach at sunset. We'll crab in the water, and walk hand-in-hand on the shore digging our toes in the wet sand. After the sun goes down, I reckon we'll find a secluded mangrove where I'll pay up on those kisses I owe you. He hoped he could connect every dot and kiss his way over every inch of her luscious body. How he would love to see the moonlight gleam on her peaches-and-cream skin. He had to encourage her diet so that he had a lot of kisses to pay up.

Remember when you, me and Jimmy used to go crabbing by the Ocean Springs Bridge? How me and Jimmy used to tease you and you kicked sand on us? Then we'd dump you in the ocean? I miss those days. I can't wait to get home and dump you in our ocean again.

You can't begin to imagine how sick I am of this infernal desert. It's dry heat with little breeze and, when there is one, it just whips sand in your face. We have to wear goggles and scarves a lot. He stopped short of describing the deadly scorpions and other nasty critters hiding beneath the sand. His leg itched where the centipede had left its calling card and he reached down to rub it. That sucker's bite had hurt a helluva lot. He couldn't begin to imagine what a scorpion sting would feel like – probably worse than stepping on a whole nest of swarming red ants. If a crab got ahold of you with its pincers, it could do some nasty business, but he was sure none of them tasted delicious like Mississippi crabs to make the tango worthwhile.

So tell me, how many kisses do I owe you?

* * * * *

"Three die in Iraq helicopter crash." Paige's heart stopped and her breath caught in her lungs.

Oh no! Danny!

She turned up the volume and stared at the newscast. Her fingernails bit so deeply into her palms they bled. "The confounded war's supposed to be over!"

Of course they didn't release the names of the victims pending notification of their families.

She took in every detail of the scene. Humvees being loaded with stretchers. Limping bloodied soldiers. Gawking nationals. Bombed out buildings.

The TV clicked off and Merline sat on her bed and hugged her. "Don't torture yourself, sugar bug. Watching all that fretful war news won't help your man. It'll just upset you."

Too late. Paige was way past upset. She hugged her roommate and took comfort from the kindness.

"What if Danny's one of them?" She couldn't envision the world without him. Even half a world away he was always very much with her.

"His parents will tell you." Merline rubbed her back consolingly.

Paige bit her lower lip to keep from blurting out, *But he's not officially my guy. They have no reason to call me.* The way she was carrying on, Merline must think she and Danny were engaged. It would be too embarrassing to admit otherwise.

Finally, she pulled away and decided to stop her pity party. Merline was right. Worrying wouldn't help Danny. Enlisting people to fill care packages and be pen pals, would.

She jogged to Tia's bungalow, needing her lieutenant's aid. By the time she banged on Tia's door, she huffed and puffed for breath.

Tia's face drained of color when she regarded Paige and ushered her inside. "Danny? Leo?"

Paige put her hand to her throat and gulped in precious air. "No. Maybe. I don't know."

Tia helped her to a tattered chair and then perched on the edge of the settee facing Paige. "*Maybe?* What happened?"

Paige wrung her hands in her lap and squeezed her eyes shut. The ringing in her ears almost deafened her. She wondered how much worse gunfire and explosions must be. A million times worse. "Probably nothing to Danny and Leo. The TV didn't give the names of the dead."

Tia gulped and blinked rapidly. She leaned forward and clasped Paige's cold hands in hers. "Back up, sweetie. Start at the beginning and tell me what happened."

Paige sucked in a big lungful of air and shifted her weight on the lumpy cushion. "A helicopter crashed in Iraq. Three US soldiers are reported dead. They didn't give their names."

"There are thousands of soldiers in Iraq," Tia said weakly, negating her brave words.

Paige stared into space, fixating on a palm frond that was scraping Tia's back window. "I know." She blinked back stinging tears. She couldn't suck enough air into her starved lungs. It was a huge effort to talk around the lump in her throat. "Whoever they were, somebody loved them."

Tia's thumb stroked Paige's hand absently. "I know. We just have to wait and pray it's not our men. And say prayers for the souls of the dead."

Paige nodded. She jumped to her feet and paced the tiny living room. "I'm going to go crazy if I just wait to hear from Danny—or his parents. I need to do something constructive."

"Let's draw up our proposals for the fund raisers. How about a car wash?" Tia took notes and they laid out their plans.

* * * * *

Paige crossed her heart before opening her post office box two days later, praying for word from Danny. Her hand shook as she turned the key and popped the door wide.

A big fat letter filled her box and she stared at it for several seconds before touching it, lest it was a mirage. She withdrew it reverently and turned it over.

Danny's scrawled handwriting greeted her and she held the letter to her heart. "Danny, be okay." This letter wasn't proof, as it had been mailed before the accident. But she still cherished it. It would be tied in the yellow ribbon with the rest of his letters and tucked away in her drawer.

Glancing at her watch she saw she was a minute late to work, so she scurried across the hall to the computer store.

"You're late!" Penny's glare scorched her. She closed out of an Internet site on the computer and then banged books around on the desk. "And now so am I. *Thanks!*"

Give me a break! Five minutes, one time.

"Some people are so inconsiderate. Some of us have a life." Penny marched out of the store, her nose so high in the air, she'd drown in a rainstorm.

Paige shook her head and settled into work. She counted the petty cash and frowned. It was off so she recounted it and still didn't find the error. She made note of it and locked the box.

Unable to get Danny and his letter off her mind, she slipped into the back room. When she slid the letter out of the envelope, a wad of names fell onto the counter.

Giddy, she felt like Christmas had just arrived early, albeit a hard candy Christmas, since Danny couldn't be here to share it with her. She pored through the names, fascinated to see where everybody was from.

Loud heels clicked behind her and she whirled around. Her heart pounded rapidly.

Penny snatched her letter from the counter and read it unashamedly. "Writing love letters on duty? To Danny?

My Danny? Danny Napolitano?" Incredulity rang out in her voice, and not a little bit of jealousy.

Paige rose to her full height and towered over the diminutive demon. She snatched the letter back. "That's private, if you don't mind. And yes, if you must know, it's Danny Napolitano, only from what I hear, he's no longer *your* Danny."

"I *do mind*. You're goofing off, leaving more work for me tomorrow. Paul should know."

Seething, Paige stepped closer into Penny's personal space. Heat suffused Paige's face. "Fine. And he should also know how often you're really late. And how you're always on the Internet during work hours."

Hatred glittered in Penny's narrowed eyes. She stomped away and flung over her shoulder, "Whatevah... It's just a crappy minimum wage work study job anyway."

Penny turned and walked backwards. "So how can you afford to send all those care packages lover boy wants?"

Paige looked pointedly at the other woman's new, expensive, high-fashion shoes. "How do you afford those?"

"None of your business." Penny pivoted on her expensive heels and smacked into Paul. Then she scurried out of the store with a mumbled, "Sorry", to their boss.

Paul adjusted his wire rim glasses and the preppy white sweater tied around his neck. Then he looked down his nose over his glasses at Paige. "What was that about?"

"Oil and vinegar," Paige mumbled, rubbing her tense forehead. "I declare. That woman is such a hypocrite! She whines and complains when I'm two minutes late, one time, when she's an hour late all the time."

Paul's brows tented. "You were late today?"

Caught by her own big mouth. Too late to hide it now plus it would be a relief that the witch couldn't dangle it over her head, she admitted, "Yes. Five minutes, tops. I'm sorry."

Should she confess to reading the letter on duty, too? *Nah.* She'd take her chances.

"Five licks with a cat o' nine tails for you, Miss Paige." Paul finger combed his hair. "Seriously, try not to be late. Everyone has schedules to keep."

And her schedule was less important than Penny's? Dumbfounded, Paige nodded, words sticking in her throat. She ambled to the back room and tucked Danny's letter away to savor later in private. It felt soiled by Penny's touch and she vowed never to give that woman another opportunity to see Danny's private words.

The afternoon dragged but closing time finally arrived and she was sprung. She found a secluded cubicle in the campus library and removed Danny's letter reverently, hoping it wasn't the last one she'd ever receive from him.

She recalled stories of her great aunt's back in World War II. Her Aunt Ruby had written faithfully to her Uncle Will who fought in Germany. Like herself and Danny, they'd been neighbors and Aunt Ruby had loved her uncle forever. Paige smiled at the happy memories. Warm and loving, they were two of her favorite people. Recently, they had celebrated their Golden Anniversary and they were globetrotting together in their golden years.

How she hoped she and Danny could follow in their footsteps!

Or would she end up like her other aunt?

Her Aunt Doris' fiancé, Bobby, had also fought in Germany during Word War II. But unlike Uncle Will, enemy fire had claimed his life, breaking her aunt's heart. Bobby had been the love of Doris' life. Although she later married Uncle Floyd, she never knew the bliss with him she had anticipated with Bobby. They'd eventually divorced.

Her Aunt Doris was just as lovely a lady as her Aunt Ruby, and just as deserving of happiness. But fate had been against Doris.

Paige prayed fate wasn't against her, too. Their family had known more than enough tragedy.

Paige pushed the old family stories aside and concentrated on Danny's letter.

"Dear Paige,

The guys all want pen pals and care packages. I hope you have enough friends to write to them or someone will be disappointed. I can only hope they'll be as lucky as me and find such a faithful pen pal."

Paige leaned back in her chair and stared at the ceiling, not really seeing it. Is that all she was to Danny? A 'faithful pen pal'? A diversion from his dreary days? Had Aunt Ruby ever felt this way? Had her stoic uncle ever written similar words?

Was she being foolish to fall in love with Danny? How pathetic was it to fixate on his words?

Paige lowered her gaze once again to Danny's words and read on.

"Promise you won't write to anyone else but me. Some of the guys asked for your address so they could write to you, too, but I told them you're all mine."

Paige's heart soared and she reread the passage several times to make sure she wasn't dreaming.

All his. Swiveling around happily, she kissed the letter. She loved the sound of being *all his.* Tingles coursed through every part of her body. If only he could be all hers, too.

She read on, eager to devour Danny's every word, to peek into his soul, to be with him in a sort of otherworldly dimension.

"How many kisses do I owe you? Ten? Twenty? I can't wait to come home and pay up. How eager are you for them? Is my motivation working?"

Her mouth grew dry and her panties became damp with anticipation of his kisses. Did she dare tell him her goal was sixty or seventy kisses? Or that she'd gained two pounds instead of losing weight? And that her big sizes were tight?

She longed for infinite kisses, not merely ten or twenty or even seventy. She yearned for the touch of his lips morning, noon and night every day for the rest of their lives. But she didn't dare confess that and scare him away.

She wondered how Aunt Ruby had reeled in Uncle Will? People in the 1940's had been a lot more prim and proper than those nowadays.

She would have to write to her aunt and ask. And she had to lose weight. Maybe if she found a higher paying job she could afford liposuction or bariatric surgery or one of those hypnosis clinics that kept sending emails. Maybe she could join a health spa and hire a private trainer.

Yeah, right. Like Hattiesburg had much employment. Nor did she have a car to travel to any nearby towns of any size.

She couldn't even afford to join Weight Warriors or e-dieting on her pitiful wages.

She reread Danny's letter four times, melting when he said he wanted to walk on moonlit Biloxi beaches with her, and find a secluded piece of beach to deliver her kisses. Reluctantly, she put it away and found her green gel pen and scalloped stationery.

"Dear Danny,

The names arrived today. I swear on my grandpa's grave that I will do my best to find pen pals for all your buddies. I can't imagine being so far away from home and not getting mail. It breaks my heart thinking about it.

We're worried about you and Leo. Honestly, how bad are things over there? The news says it's worse now than ever. They're reporting that more men are dying. I thought the war was over? That your troops were there to keep the peace? I pray you weren't hurt...or worse. I don't know what I'd do if anything happened to you."

Chills raced up her spine and she huddled into her sweater. She tucked a few stray hairs behind her ears but they insisted on spilling onto her letter.

"I can't wait for you to come home—or pay up on the kisses you owe me, either."

She chewed the end of her pen as she debated whether to confess the truth about her weight gain. He might think she didn't want his kisses and she never wanted him to think that.

"You owe me five kisses."

She was going to burn in hell. She'd just have to dig in and truly lose the weight before he got home.

"When do you get to come home and deliver them?"

She prayed soon. With much reluctance, she forced herself back to the real world of books, college and students.

"What do you want in your care package? I didn't see it on the list.

Love,

Paige"

She sealed the letter with a kiss. Then she wrote a second one to her aunt.

"Dear Aunt Ruby,

Remember how you told me that you wrote to Uncle Will when he was in Germany during WW II?

Might I ask if that's how you fell in love with each other? Or what you did to make Uncle Will fall in love with you?"

Of course Ruby was gorgeous, warm and kind. All the men must have been in love with her.

She finished the letter with the normal pleasantries, asking after their current trip to Scotland.

After she posted the letters, she hunted Tia down, and found her in the Student Union sipping tea and reading a book.

"Hi y'all." Paige waved Danny's letter under her friend's nose. "We've got the names now."

Tia took the envelope and withdrew the list. She whistled loudly when she saw how long it was. "We'd best get working on it."

"Great minds think alike. Come on." Paige couldn't stand the delicious smells another moment before she attacked a big juicy cheeseburger.

"Chill. We can work here." Tia sipped her tea gingerly making no move to leave.

Paige scowled. "Not if I don't want to tackle the snack bar. I'm gaining, not losing weight."

Tia's teacup chinked against the saucer when she put it down so that some of the brew sloshed over the rim, pooling in the saucer. "What kind of fruit do you like?"

Huh? "Apples. Watermelon. Bananas. Strawberries. And fried plantains." Her favorite. A pitifully small assortment, which accounted for a lot of her eating problems.

"No more fried anything for you, girlfriend. I'm your new personal trainer. You'll eat what and when I say." Tia scraped her chair back from the table and she stood up. "Sit your buns here and don't move."

Paige almost saluted and retorted, *'Yes, ma'am,'* but bit her tongue. Her forehead furrowed, she watched her new drill instructor march to the snack bar. Danny wasn't the only one who'd been drafted into the military it seemed.

Tia returned with a MacIntosh apple, a blueberry yogurt and a carton of fat free milk. When she ordered, "Eat that," the "Rocky" theme song played in Paige's mind.

Cross-eyed, Paige stared at the selection. "That's not enough to keep a flea alive."

Tia sighed as she took her seat and dug into her own salad. "Do you want to complain? Or lose weight?"

Of course she wanted to lose weight! But did it have to involve torture? Starvation? "Lose weight," she grumbled as she put a hex on the fat free milk. "I'm sure Danny and Leo are eating better than this." *Without the care packages.*

"Complain, complain, complain. Save it for when we're jogging two miles at dawn every morning." Tia slid her a maliciously gleeful look.

"That's cruel and inhumane punishment. I'll throw up." Horrified, Paige cast a quick glance at her new DI. *Jog* wasn't in her vocabulary. It had to be the worst word in the English language, next to *run*.

"Okay. We'll start with calisthenics and run half a mile to build you up." Tia picked a cherry tomato out of her salad and popped it into her mouth. Then she waved the dressing-coated fork at her. "No pain, no gain. If you want to lose weight—and earn lots of kisses—you have to exercise and eat right. Surely you want Danny's kisses more than a cheeseburger and fries. Or maybe you belong in a loony bin."

"You don't even cast a shadow so how can you understand?" Paige's stomach fussed at her for nourishment. Grudgingly, she took a bite of the apple and chewed it.

"Seriously—you have to decide which one you want most. Danny or food." Annoyance flickered across her friend's dark eyes as if Paige was losing her mind.

Danny, of course! At least that's what her heart and mind screamed. Her stomach fought back.

"Finish that and we'll take our run now. Exercise will curb your hunger. You'll see." Tia pushed her bowl away and dabbed her mouth with a napkin.

"But it's evening! You said *dawn*." It wasn't fair to blindside her and inflict the torture early.

"Exercise now and I guarantee you won't want to attack a midnight snack."

"Of course not. I'll be dead." Or at least too tired and sore to do anything but stretch out on her bed with heating pads under both legs.

Tia rolled her eyes. "If it works… Finish up. My Nikes are calling me."

Paige stared at her poor brainless friend. "You're demented."

"I'm in shape and I'll help you if it kills us both."

"It just might…" Paige said in a singsong voice. The stupid "Rocky" song wouldn't shut up and she gave in and hummed along.

* * * * *

The phone shrilled in the middle of the night. Paige couldn't pry her eyes open so she felt around for the horrid instrument, swearing silently. Something demonic crashed to the floor with a loud bang.

Merline's bed squeaked loudly. "Lord almighty. What misguided soul would be calling at five a.m.?"

"A demon," Paige mumbled as she lifted the wicked receiver. "Go back to sleep."

"I heard that!" Tia screeched in her ear. "Rise and shine. The sun's up and you have a hot date with the pavement."

Paige almost slammed down the phone.

As if psychic, Tia warned, "Don't you dare hang up or I'll pound on your door and drag you out of bed."

"The pavement will still be there this evening. Catch me after class." *Better yet, don't catch her anytime.* Running at any hour was pure torture. Ask her aching calves, which were making love to the heating pads.

"Uh-uh. You're not squirming out of this. You're going to be thin and gorgeous when Danny returns if it kills me. You'll thank me."

"You mean if it kills me." She wanted to execute her absurdly upbeat friend. No one liked these hours, except maybe Polar Bear swimmers and they were nuts.

"One more objection and I'm adding a mile to your run."

"Hitler," Paige murmured, turning off the lovely heating pads and unplugging them. "My muscles hate you."

"How bad are they?" Concern etched Tia's voice. "You don't have any charlie horses, do you?"

Paige considered lying, but couldn't. She massaged her sore legs, holding the wireless phone to her ear with her shoulder. "Not that bad. Just achy."

"That's a good burn. Means your muscles are getting a workout. We just need to warm up and cool off properly. Meet me at the end of Fraternity Row in fifteen minutes."

"Aye aye, Captain." This time, Paige did salute the phone after she hung up.

"You're both insane," Merline said on a big yawn. She snuggled back under her covers and lowered her sleeping eye patch over her face again. "She's not going to call here at five a.m. every morning, is she? I need my beauty rest."

"God, I hope not." But Tia was mule-headed and didn't pay any heed to convention.

Paige stood and stretched her arms high over her head, yawning loudly. Then she threw the cover over her pillow. She'd straighten the spread out later. Maybe she'd get back in time to sleep awhile before her first class at nine. No use making up a perfectly comfortable bed for a few minutes' insanity.

She shrugged into her comfortable worn sweat suit, the jade one that used to match her eyes before it became faded from a hundred washings. Then she slipped into her deck shoes and she pulled her long hair back into a high ponytail to keep it off her neck.

Taking only her key, she strolled to the end of Fraternity Row, muttering under her breath. The moon was still visible. No one woke up before the sun.

Her arms crossed over her small chest, her toe tapping, Tia regarded her with a shake of her head. "You'll have to move faster than that to whittle your waist. And you need better running shoes."

"Now who's complaining?" Birds sang beautifully. Dewdrops slid down springy blades of grass. A slight breeze ruffled her hair, tickling her neck. "I didn't know birds could sing so beautifully."

Tia snorted. "I'm allowed to correct you. I'm your trainer." She looked up at a family of birds in the shady pecan tree.

"First, we warm up so your legs won't get sore. You don't want to get a charlie horse." Tia bent and touched her toes. "Do what I do."

Paige followed her lead, twisting and turning in inhumane ways. The push-ups were the worst. She couldn't push her body off the ground to save her life and she was getting way too intimate with the pesky gravel and sharp rocks.

Tia slid her a sideways glance as she drew herself to her feet. "You really haven't heard the birds sing like this? What planet have you been on? The birds always sing early in the morning."

"Planet Moonlight," Paige said, not skipping a beat. Maybe mornings weren't the devil incarnate. She loved the birds' serenade and absence of noise to drown them out.

Tia jogged in place and balled her fists. Her glossy black braid bounced between her shoulder blades. "Come on, Dracula. It's time to discover there is life in the sunlight."

"'Dracula'? I'll get you for that. You'd better run fast."

"Like a gazelle. Catch me if you can."

Tia outdistanced her easily, and ran two blocks ahead before she turned around to glare at Paige. "You're supposed to run."

Paige loped, the stitch in her stomach paining her. She held her side, gasping for air. "I am running. I'm not the tri-athlete you are. I need to work my way up to two miles." Much more of this and she was going to toss her stomach. Luckily she hadn't eaten breakfast yet.

"Good thing you're not in the Army. You'd have a D.I. yelling at you to move those buns." Tia glowered at her as if she were a drill instructor.

Paige caught up to her friend and shook her ponytail behind her.

It's a good hurt. Burning is good. Paige chanted the unbelievable mantra in her mind the rest of the day as her tax professor droned through his lecture. Didn't the man ever tweeze his graying, bushy unibrow? She amused herself and tried to take her mind off her achy legs by counting how many corkscrew wiry hairs wound their way out.

Her legs gimpy, she hobbled to her classes and then to the store. *It's a good hurt. The burn is good,* she chanted silently.

Tia was waiting for her with a bag of carrots and an apple. "Reinforcements. In case you forgot."

"Dare I accept apples from the queen?"

"Watch it," Tia glared at her and perched on the edge of her desk, so tiny and pretty Paige was about to gag. She extracted a carrot and nibbled it, her nose twitching. "I'm on your side, remember."

"I get grumpy when I'm roused before the rooster."

"Okay. So no more fighting each other. We're a team. Pact?"

"Yep." Paige took the apple and polished it on her shirt. "Thanks." Apples she could do. Carrots were bland without the dip so she left them on the edge of her desk as she bit into the fruit. Luscious juice dribbled down her chin and she dabbed at it with a napkin.

Tia walked around and opened the desk drawers without asking, and poked around unabashedly.

"What are you doing?" Paige worried that Paul or someone would see her friend in the off-limits location and think the worst.

"Looking for contraband." At Paige's quirked brow, Tia said, "You know. Candy. Chocolate. Chips. Fattening stuff."

Paige's mouth watered at the mention of chocolate. She crossed her heart solemnly. "If any is in there, it's not mine. I'm not the only one who uses this desk. You really shouldn't…"

"Why are you rifling through our drawers?" Penny marched up to them, and slammed the drawer, almost catching Tia's fingers. "Employees only."

Tia jerked back, her eyes widening in surprise. "I was just making sure my friend wasn't hiding food."

"You could get your friend fired for going through our private desk." Penny anchored her hands on her slim, almost boyish hips and glowered at her. "Why are you permitting it? You well know there are confidential documents in there. Petty cash. Bank statements."

Defensive, Paige rose to her feet and snapped back, "She didn't know and I was just trying to tell her that when you so kindly interrupted me."

"So what are you hiding?" Penny rounded the desk, shoved her way between them and looked through the drawers one by one.

"Nothing," Paige said on a long sigh, pushing stray locks of hair behind her ears, her freckles baking in her heat-suffused cheeks.

Penny sauntered to the back office and sat down at the computer. "Right and I'm a leprechaun."

"Witch," Tia said loudly, fury glittering in her darkened eyes. She hitched her purse higher on her shoulder. "We're having a rally tonight about the soldiers at the Alpha Psi house. We'll be assigning names."

"Tonight! Why didn't you tell me?"

"I am. They just told me, sweetie, and I hiked it on over here to fill you in." Tia backed out the doorway into the main store. "I'll meet you here at closing and we'll catch a bite to eat before the meeting."

Most likely a bite was all Tia would let her ingest. Paige's stomach gnawed at her so she took another bite of the apple, the carrots beginning to look immensely better than they had a few mere minutes before.

* * * * *

A dust cloud kicked up on the horizon. Knots tightening in his stomach, Danny chewed on his licorice and watched the cloud grow larger. With all the suicide bombings and ambushes, everything was suspect in this neck of the woods.

"Maybe that's the convoy over yonder," Leo said, pointing at it. He drew his lanky length up and shielded his eyes from the brutal sun. "I sure hope it's bringing mail from home."

"You mean mail from the girls." Danny lived for mail from Paige. As much as Danny longed for more word from her, his stomach never settled until he was sure the approaching vehicle was friendly. He did not want to be sent home in a body bag or missing a leg. He hoped to return just as fit as when he arrived. He worried that, even if his body returned without scars, his psyche would never forget some of the terror he'd witnessed.

"Yep. I'm thinking of asking for that little filly's hand. I didn't know it was possible to fall in love through the mail."

"People meet on the Internet and get married all the time. Same difference." Acute longing blindsided him. He missed his computer and electronics workshop in his attic.

"I always thought that sounded a mite crazy. Only lonely people do that." Leo scratched his head. "Guess we're a mite lonely."

Danny looked at his buddy crosswise. "Speak for yourself, bubba. I'm not lonely. I have you."

Leo shoved him jovially, almost pushing him down into the sand. "That's not the kind of lonely I was speaking of, pardner."

Leastways, it better not be.

* * * * *

Tia barged into Paige's room without so much as a knock, her step light and airy, an ear-to-ear grin lighting up her face. "Here's an early Christmas present," Tia said beaming at Paige and held out an envelope.

Really early, bless her soul. "Thanks." Paige tore it open and spied a Weight Warrior's gift certificate. She couldn't think of a better present, except for Danny to return home.

Excitement humming in her veins, Paige leapt to her feet and hugged the angel. "You're the best. What would I do without you?"

"You're never going to have to find out as I'm not going anywhere. Go get started." Tia nudged her to the computer.

Signing into the Weight Warrior's site took only a few seconds. Intrigued by the many articles and advice, Paige surfed the enormous site.

"Check out the recipes," Tia said, leaning over her shoulder.

"Yum! Diet pumpkin pie." Paige's mouth watered. She printed out the recipe. "I'm borrowing your kitchen."

"My kitchen es su kitchen. Make enough for two and you got a deal."

"Deal." They shook on it as Paige's stomach growled. "Ooh! This vegetable gumbo has practically no calories. I can do this."

"Veggies are good. Just remember your proteins and carbs. You don't want to go into starvation mode, either." Tia's narrowed eyes reflected on the monitor.

Paige laughed and shook her head. "Fat chance." She snatched the gumbo recipe from the printer and made her way to the kitchen where she raided Tia's vegetable bin.

A frown pinched Paige's brow as she backtracked. "You said carbs? I thought they were bad for you."

"There are good carbs. Read the article on the site. It'll tell you."

The TV suddenly seemed to blare from the living room. "...Four soldiers are reported dead after this morning's early bombing of Kav. Five others are reported injured, in critical condition."

Paige's heart lurched and she froze. The knife in her hand clattered to the floor. "Danny!" Her breath trapped in her chest as she spun on her heel and fled to the living room.

White-faced, Tia stared at the television as she wrung her hands in her lap. "They never announce the victims' names this soon." The raw emotion lacing her friend's voice matched that tearing apart her heart.

Paige hugged her friend, trying to give comfort, as she struggled for breath. "I need to know, too."

Tia drew back and gazed at her pityingly. "You truly love him, don't you?"

Her love for Danny swept her away with tidal wave force, almost drowning her in its strength. Her tongue thick and awkward, she nodded. "I've always loved him. Or at least I thought so. But these past few months, writing to him..." *Baring her soul, looking deeply into his, her heart had swollen a hundred times its original size.*

"Is it possible to fall in love through letters?" Tia wrung her hands in her lap as she gazed up at Paige, with utter heartbreak etched across her face. "Are we crazy?"

We? Paige's heart went out to her friend and sister. "You, too? Maybe we're both crazy."

Tia tossed her a slight, lopsided smile, a ghost of her usual self. "Not you. You actually knew Danny before you started corresponding. I've never met Leo face-to-face. Never kissed him…and now he might be…" A broken sob escaped her trembling lips.

Paige watched the drama unfolding half a world away with horror as chaos reigned around wounded, shell-shocked soldiers. The surreal scene looked like an old war movie inside the television but it was all too real. The man she loved could be injured—or dead—and she hadn't even told him she loved him. *No! Life couldn't be so unfair.*

Since when was war fair?

She mumbled for her friend's benefit, "People meet and fall in love over the Internet every day. Why can't we do it the old-fashioned way with pen and ink? Our souls mate so that we're not enamored by superficial things like appearance." Not that any man who gazed upon the fair Tia wouldn't fall deeply, madly in love with her.

Tia curled her freezing fingers around Paige's and squeezed hard. "You're such a sweetie, no wonder I chose you to be my sister."

Not that Paige wished heartbreak on her closest friend, but she took a small measure of comfort in the camaraderie.

Tia pursed her lips and rose to her feet. She punched the TV remote ferociously, turning off the news. "It won't help us to dwell on it. What were we doing?"

"Fixing lunch." Paige's stomach clenched, rebelling at the thought of food at such a time. "I can't eat."

The tiny bungalow felt impossibly small and suffocating. "Let's get out of here." *Away from the devilish box that only delivered bad news.*

Tia nodded, blinking back tears that clung to her long lashes. "Maybe a workout will relieve some tension." Could anything, save news that her Danny was safe, relieve her fears? Not likely, but anything was better than staring at the war-torn soldiers.

She lifted silent prayers that their men were alive and safe. A momentary flash of anger assailed her. *Why did you have to enlist and put yourself in danger?*

Immediate shame flooded her and she chastised herself. Danny and his comrades were making noble sacrifices for her ungrateful soul. She didn't deserve him even if by some miracle he wanted her.

Tia slipped into her room and came out in a flowery beach wrap. "I want to swim laps 'til I'm too tired to think."

Excellent idea! If only she could escape the demons torturing her so unmercifully. Hopefully, she could drown out their tormenting whispers. "I'll meet you at the Aquatics Center soon as I get my swimsuit."

Tia locked the house and then linked her arm through Paige's. "Oh, no. I don't want to be alone with my thoughts. We'll stick together."

Paige nodded, wondering what she had ever done to merit such a true friend. Fallen pecans crunched underfoot as they picked up their pace. "Let's go."

* * * * *

Scowling, swearing under his breath, Danny wiped the grime from his dusty face. Suarez, Washington and Nguyen were gone. Two left young children behind.

Burying fallen comrades was pure, agonizing hell. Writing condolence letters to their families would be worse. Their blood literally stained his hands as he lifted their lifeless bodies onto stretchers. At a mere nineteen years of age, Nguyen had left a small daughter with her parents. Washington left three children and a loving widow. Danny tried to shield his heart from the excruciating pain but wasn't enough of an iceman to shut it out, so that the pain slashed it to ribbons.

What if he was on one of those stretchers, his arms folded across his chest, the blanket covering his face? How much would his loved ones suffer? Paige? Thank God he didn't have a wife and children to leave behind should he fall prey to enemy fire. Better that he die alone than leave a grieving wife.

Paige's latest letter burned through his shirt pocket to his heart. He had to end whatever it was happening between them before she got hurt. He couldn't bear the thought of causing her so much despair. He cursed himself for letting their harmless friendship grow into something deeper.

The thought of pushing her away when he needed her so badly, turned him inside out but it had to be done. Raw and exhausted, he wondered where he'd find the strength. She was his lifeline in this godforsaken hell.

Leo picked up the opposite end of the stretcher and they carried it to the waiting humvee. After the medic checked the dog tags and zipped the body bag, they saluted their fallen brethren. "I don't envy you, having to write to her family. How do you tell a little girl her mama's gone up to live with the angels?"

Depressed, Danny grimaced as he hauled himself into his truck and fell into place in the convoy, hating his job more than ever. He swore he'd never complain about tax season again if he made it home in one piece. It might be boring, and the clients could be very demanding but no bullets would be flying and he'd be inside a plush office surrounded by cool, sweet air conditioning. "Maybe you should write the letter. You have a better way with words."

Leo's lips twisted wryly and he wiped his palms down his fatigues. "I don't envy you, man. I wouldn't want your job."

"Some job," Danny agreed, muttering, feeling a thousand times Scroogier than Ebenezer. Some Christmas letter he'd be sending home to that little girl. *Duty sucked.* The truck Danny was driving tipped to the right and the tires spun. He gritted his teeth and revved the engine but all he accomplished was a big mushroom cloud that the enemy could see from miles away. "Damn! She won't budge."

"Just dandy." Leo snatched the radio and called, "Mayday. Assistance needed. Our truck is stuck in the sand." He whipped off his hat and wiped the perspiration from his brow.

The convoy rolled on ahead of them, apparently not noticing they had fallen back, and Danny swore under his breath again as he jumped out of the truck to inspect the damage. The front right tire was almost completely buried and the rear tire sunk fast. Frustrated, he kicked the lousy thing. It could take hours to dig them out and he wasn't comfortable sticking around this place for an extra five minutes much less several hours. They might as well dig their own grave. Innocent looking civilians could be suicide bombers and snipers lived to pick them off with no more remorse than if they were picking tin cans off fence rails.

One lone truck brought up the rear, and rolled to a stop beside them. A private first class yelled out her window, "You need assistance, Captain?"

"We could sure use some strong backs. Looks like this baby'll have to be dug out." Danny grimaced, the brutal African sun assaulting his eyes despite his dark shades. The glare reflected off the endless sea of sand so that looking away from the glowing orb did little to help soothe his burning eyes.

"You got it." The engine rumbled to a stop and five or six soldiers alighted from the vehicle. They fished around in the back of the truck and found a couple of shovels, which were almost as valuable as weapons in this part of the world.

Leo bounced on his haunches and pulled his cap back on his head as he inspected the tires and rolled his infernal toothpick around in his mouth. "When we leave here, I never want to see another grain of sand. I got sand in places I don't want to know about."

"Easy for you to say, mountain man. My job's waiting on Biloxi Beach. Long as I can feel the ocean breeze and smell those shrimp, I'll be right as rain." Danny pulled a couple of pieces of licorice out of his pocket and handed one to the cowboy. With the candy dangling from his mouth, he started scooping sand away from the tires. They needed something to provide friction for the tires to grab or they would just keep spinning until they reached the earth's core.

"I sure do miss my mountains. After this, I'll never complain about snow again. Think I'll see if Tia will go skiing with me. There's some great slopes up by my hunting lodge. They have a waiting list for their honeymoon suite…"

Danny glanced at his buddy in surprise and quickly masked his disapproval. Leo had marriage to Tia on the brain? He'd only been corresponding with her for a couple of months and he hadn't met her in person yet. *Damn that was quick and irresponsible!*

They have a couple honeymoon suites. Maybe you and Paige can rent the other one?" Pure cussedness twinkled in the cowboy's eyes.

Despite his well-meaning resolve, images of Paige naked, sprawled on the round double king-sized bed teased him unmercifully. Slick with his lovemaking, she'd slide over black satin sheets and her fabulous red hair, alight with sexy blond highlights, would be fanned out behind her on the pillows. He was on fire for her. If he made it home alive, he'd keep her in that bed a solid week! Maybe more.

Gunfire rang out of nowhere and bullets whizzed by Danny's face.

"Shit, soldier! Take cover behind the vehicles now!"

Bombs exploded nearby. "Guess no one told those scoundrels the freakin' war is officially over," Leo said, scrambling on his hands and knees in the sand.

"Just a technicality, bubba. Look around and tell me it's over." Another bomb exploded and Danny shielded his eyes. His ears rang with the impact as the truck rocked alarmingly, almost turning over on them.

"If we manage to get out of this hell hole, I'm gonna bury myself in my lady and never let her go."

Where in the hell was their unit? They should have come back for them by now...unless they'd ridden into an ambush and couldn't return.

"Look out!" Leo yelled as a bomb burst in front of the jeep, hurling them several yards.

Shrapnel pierced Danny's thigh and excruciating pain burst through him. Screams gurgled in his throat as terrifying blackness overtook him.

Chapter Six

Paige's robe pooled around her feet and she said a quick prayer and stepped on the scale. It wasn't her official weigh-in day but she had become obsessed with her weight, which she checked every morning and evening even though she knew only the morning weigh-in reflected an accurate weight.

Good! A pound lighter from the previous day. According to her weight loss program, she should only lose two pounds a week but she was impatient. She wanted to be slim and gorgeous by the time Danny came home. At the very least she wanted a washboard stomach. Focusing on her weight also helped her not to worry as much about the danger he might be in, although nothing could completely alleviate her concern. She'd hold her breath 'til the day Danny stepped back on American soil, safe and sound.

Eager to get in her exercise, she slid into her jogging suit. It was getting baggy and, although it was the drawstring variety, it still tented around her legs. Time to trade it in for a smaller size.

Man did she love it!

Happy and whistling, she rang up Tia. "Wake up, sleeping beauty. Jogging time. I'll meet you in front of your place."

Tia groaned. "Go back to sleep, Frankenstein. The roosters aren't even crowing yet." Sleep crowded her friend's voice as she yawned profusely.

Paige ignored her friend's grumpiness just as Tia had ignored all her early protests. *Bless her tired soul, jogging would get the blood flowing through her veins.* "You've got fifteen minutes."

She jogged around fraternity row twice, keeping an eye on the time. She didn't get breathless anymore and she loved the early morning invigorating chill and the blooming magnolias. How she loved Mississippi and the campus, especially when the new day was dawning. The magnificent sunrise stole her breath as it bathed the university in its pastel light. She'd have to bring a camera the next morning and snap some pictures to send to Danny. He'd always loved the campus, too.

Acute longing for Danny beset her. How she wished he were here to share it with her. They could jog together and enjoy every sunrise and sunset and then make long, languorous love under the Mississippi moon. *Pure heaven.*

Tingles that were impossible to quell shimmied down her body. Danny couldn't come home too soon. A shooting star blazed across the early morning sky and she hugged herself and wished for Danny to come home soon.

She watched the spectacular sight in awe until its shimmering dust dissipated in the brightening sunlight.

* * * * *

Paige took a big bite out of her apple as she sat at the Alpha Psi table, signing up volunteers to correspond with the soldiers. Then she took a sip of her bottled water during the next lull in volunteers. Delighted that she found the water more and more satisfying as the craving for sugary sodas diminished, she took another swig of water. It actually helped fill her up now so that she didn't feel the urge to attack the snack vending machine between meals. To be on the safe side, she also kept a couple extra apples and a bag of cut-up radishes in her book bag for those times she became famished. So what if people looked at her strangely when she popped a radish into her mouth. Her new size fourteens were getting baggy and she was fitting into several medium sizes.

Humming happily, the day zipped by as Paige told classmates and the staff about Danny and his pals.

Around three p.m. after her final class of the day, Tia dropped her book bag on the table and plopped into the vacant seat beside Paige. "How's it going?"

A happy twinkle in her eyes, Paige nearly shouted. "Over three hundred people so far signed up to be pen pals and we've collected at least a few hundred dollars." She patted the steel petty cash box with pride swelling in her heart.

"Cool beans. That'll cover all the soldiers in the guys' unit plus some."

Enthusing to her favorite subject, joy swelling in her heart, Paige shook her head emphatically. "I can't wait to tell Danny. We have a pen pal for every single name he sent to me."

"Awesome, dudette. Leo'll be hollering and jumping up and down for joy, too." Tia counted the money, wonder in her eyes. "There's almost a thousand dollars here! I feel a shopping trip coming on. I have to tell Neresa and Melanie Jo." She whipped out her cell phone and called the Alpha Psi house, gushing the wonderful news.

Paige listened shamelessly as she played the hostess with the mostest, schmoozing more students and faculty to join their cause. Patriotism ran high and several more people joined their ranks, eager to do their part for the soldiers.

Only a couple voiced any protest about the war and the US presence in Iraq. Just one called her a warmonger. She did her best to swallow the insult and move on with her mission, assured she was helping men and women like Danny who were sacrificing so much to keep America safe.

When Tia put the phone away in her purse, she said, "I've got it handled. Neresa is coming to deposit the money and take the names back to the Alpha Psi house. You're sprung."

Paige wanted to get a bike ride in before sunset. She could taste that size twelve and itched to clear her closet of the larger sizes. She couldn't wait to take her size fourteens to the consignment shop.

"Thanks!" She gave her friend a peck on the cheek, hoisted her book bag over her shoulder and then hiked it across campus to her dorm. She crunched on the rest of her apple as she walked. She hoped eating apples really helped to burn calories. That's what the article claimed that she'd just read.

She dumped her books on her bed, tucked her keys and cell phone into her pockets and then whistled the "Rocky" theme song as she made her way outside to the bike rack. What a glorious fall day to ride her bike! The crisp, cool air exhilarated her as the late afternoon sun warmed her back.

She pedaled around campus three times and then struck out towards the Hattiesburg zoo. She loved to visit the animals, especially the beautiful big cats that possessed the grace she hoped to achieve. It still amazed her that such a small town had its own zoo when her larger home city of Biloxi-Gulfport, did not. It was only one of the many things she loved about her adopted Hattiesburg, even if Biloxi would always hold first place in her heart.

She chained her bike to a rack not far from the zoo, and checked her watch to see how long she'd been riding. Not bad—seventy minutes. The delicious ache in her thighs let her know the exercise was doing its job. Pleased, she calculated that the ride would give her a good five activity points for the day, not counting her treks to class and back.

Thirsty, she took a swig of her bottled water. Hot and sweaty, she splashed a bit onto her hands and rubbed it over her face and arms.

Ah! Much better.

She dropped a few coins in the feeding machines and purchased some feed for the animals. Soon a family of ducks waddled after her as she alternated tossing food to them and the confined animals.

She paused longest in front of the lions and tigers, drinking in their svelte beauty. She particularly loved the leopards, which were spotted like her, so that she felt an odd kinship of sorts. If they could live so well in their spotted hide, so could she.

She ambled around the zoo 'til dusk when her watch warned her that she need go to the cafeteria now or pay her own dime for dinner, not that she was all that hungry. It seemed the more she stayed active, the less hungry she felt. But if she didn't eat now, she feared she'd be starved by bedtime and then attack everything in sight, probably the easiest and worst foods for her diet.

"Bye guys." She waved to her leopards and worried when the ducks followed her, honking, demanding more food she didn't have.

She washed down a grilled chicken and tomato pita with a diet iced tea and followed it up with a fat free mint ice cream sandwich. Then she slipped out into the gorgeous starlit evening. The heavens never failed to stun her with their glittering beauty and she wondered if Danny could see the same stars as she. She comforted herself knowing he could see the same moon.

Calculating Iraq time off the top of her head, she knew he'd be closer to daybreak than the delectable sunset she'd just witnessed biking home. Acute longing for Danny assailed her. She'd not received a letter from him in nearly a week. She prayed he hadn't suffered a change of heart about their friendship. She tasted Heaven in his letters and she didn't want to give that up — ever.

Her longing for Danny worried her and she chastised herself for letting her guard so far down. In attempting to seduce him, she'd sprung a trap for herself. Infatuation and hero worship from afar was one thing, but unrequited love another. Maybe she was a fool for revealing her heart and her lust so openly. She wasn't Tia who could flutter her lashes and charm a hundred men. She doubted she'd have that effect on men even if she were to shrink to a size four, forget the ten.

Still, she couldn't wait to tell Danny what an overwhelming success Operation Pen Pal had been and that, very soon, all the men and women in his outfit would receive their first letters and care packages. Needing the solitude that was impossible to find in her room when Merline was around, she stretched out beneath an ancient oak tree after she ascertained it wasn't infested with red ants or other pesky critters.

In a purple mood, she set her pen to purple ink and wrote.

"Dear Danny,

Awesome news! I signed up 334 people to be pen pals and collected over $1,000.00 for care packages today. Tia's itching to start shopping LOL. Well, so am I. I hate to think of y'all going without the essentials.

I lost three more pounds this week and I'm down to a size twelve. Size ten here I come! Woo hoo! I'm so pumped. I took my bike out for a spin earlier and wound up at the zoo. I'll have to take you to see it when you get home and introduce you to my leopards."

Now, for the hard part, which she debated committing to paper since she detected reticence on his part. She chewed the end of her pen while she pondered her next words carefully. Feeling earthier, not as high on life, she clicked over to the green ink. It was better than black, which might indicate too well how morose this subject made her feel.

"I've been watching the news reports and it seems there are more and more attacks on our troops, not less like I would've expected since the war's been officially declared over for months. What's really happening over there? Be honest with me, just how much danger are you in?"

She paused, staring at the word *danger* for so long it seemed to vibrate before her eyes. It came alive, mocking her, downright frightening her.

"Why are more troops being sent over? Does that mean you'll be rotating home soon? God I hope so!

Have I told you how proud I am of you for serving like this? For representing all of us? I've been wondering if I should enlist and take my turn. It's not fair for you to be there, and not me."

She debated wadding up the letter and deleting that section and then decided to leave it. It wasn't like the war was a secret to him and he must know they'd get news reports back home. He also had to know any sane person who cared as much as an inkling for him would entertain at least some worries on his behalf.

But she didn't want to leave him in a gloomy mood either, so she forced herself to sound perkier and change the subject. She switched to red ink, taking a chance it wouldn't scare him away.

L'amore humming through her veins and making her pulse skitter, she continued writing.

"I hope you're keeping tally as I am. Add three more kisses for a total of thirty-one."

Her pussy quivered at the thought of thirty-one long, sensual, hot kisses, of being held in Danny's arms and feeling his lips plunder hers. Surely within the magical space of thirty-one kisses, he would hunger for more than merely ravaging her lips and seek even greater treasures. It was all she could do not to rub her hot mons over the ground for release. Only the thought of someone seeing her from a window above kept her in check. She'd have to find a thoroughly secluded place, out of sight of anyone, to write her next love letter to Danny.

Would the thought of thirty-one kisses excite him as it did her? She hoped so.

She signed off quickly, needing a freezing shower before she instantaneously combusted and took the poor old tree with her. But she couldn't resist adding a P.S.

"P.S. I ordered some fur-lined handcuffs online last night."

She thought better of adding that she'd also bought white fur pasties and a couple of huge plumes...

* * * * *

"I can't do *that!*" Shocked and majorly embarrassed, Paige backed herself into a literal corner, her eyes wide and disbelieving. She had heard Key West's Fantasy Fest was wild, that everyone dressed in costume, but she'd never dreamed it was *this* wild. She should have checked it out more thoroughly before letting Tia drag her into something so totally wild.

Completely naked, her legs spread wide, Tia smiled at her. "Chicken? Everybody gets painted. You'll stand out more if you don't."

The airbrush artist sprayed gold paint over Tia's Brazilian-waxed pussy. Half-turning to her, his face not two inches from Tia's elongated nipples, he said, "There's nothing to be scared of. See? You won't look naked once I paint you."

"Then what's the point?" Paige crossed her arms tightly over her chest, protecting it. She knew it was silly, as she was fully clothed and the man didn't have x-ray vision, but it made her feel a bit more protected, nonetheless.

Tia glared at her. "To let loose and feel free! To celebrate your new body. Do this and I guarantee you'll feel more comfortable in your skin. Come on. I'm doing it, too. We can be a matched set. I'm going to be a lion. You can be a tiger."

She couldn't deny that she was very happy with her new figure. More than fifty pounds lighter and seven sizes smaller, it would be a helluva way to celebrate her weight loss victory. Every time she looked in the mirror now, she could hardly believe she was looking at herself. She looked like a new person. Better yet, she felt so very wonderful.

"We can wear masks and no one will know who we are. Promise." Tia's lion took shape and she looked gorgeous. Except for her beaded nipples, she looked completely covered.

"Amazing, don't you think?" the artist said with a twinkle in his green eyes. "You would make an amazing tiger. Let me paint you."

"It's on me," Tia said hurriedly. She put her mask on. "See? No one will know who you are, except me and thee. You can't fully experience Festival without getting in costume."

"Mademoiselle is right. It's not the same. I'll make you a stunning tigress." The goateed man looked expectantly up at her. If he licked his lips, she was so out of here.

If he licked his lips, she was so out of here.

Her resolve wavered. She'd always wanted to be a tigress and this was her chance. She chewed her lower lips. "But isn't it illegal to go outside naked?"

The French man shook his head, a twinkle in his eyes. "*Mais non.* Not during festival. All the women do it."

"Not the men?" Festival sounded very sexist. So the men got to look their fill but she didn't?

"I paint men, too." He pointed to several pictures in his photo gallery. All the men wore shorts or slacks. Only their bare chests were painted.

"We're holding up Francois' business. Decide now. You'll regret it if you don't," Tia said, *soto voce*.

Paige's pussy tingled at the thought of parading around the streets naked except for a painted-on costume. "So this is why you talked me into the Brazilian wax job."

Tia's grin widened. "Of course, darling. Do it *pour moi*. Friends don't let friends stroll around naked alone."

Despite herself, Paige chuckled at the outrageous logic. It would serve Tia right if she let her do just that. But strolling around naked sounded so delicious she feared she would regret not joining in the fun. Would she ever get another opportunity to parade in front of other people sans clothing? It was the stuff her fantasies were made of. It wasn't like she visited Key West all the time. This was her first, and perhaps her only, trip. It was hell and gone from Mississippi so no one would recognize her, especially not wearing the mask. And it would be a celebration of her svelte new figure as Tia had said. "Okay. Do it fast before I chicken out."

Tia purred and stretched her limbs languidly. "You'll love it. I do."

She hoped the night would be warm. She'd never paraded around nude outside before, and never in front of a mob of strangers, inside or out.

"Don't be shy. This is what I do. I see thousands of naked women. This is art, not sex."

Closing her eyes, she chanted to herself, "this is art, not sex" as she disrobed and stood naked before the hulking stranger.

"A true redhead," the artist said in awe. "Quite rare."

Her pussy quivered as he spread her thighs wide and began painting stripes up her legs. "How can you tell? I'm completely waxed." Not a red curly hair remained on her mons. She'd checked.

"All your freckles. Your boyfriend must love them."

She wouldn't know and worried they would repulse Danny if he ever gazed upon her unclothed. However, this unexpected praise bolstered her ego.

The artist gazed upon her critically as he worked his way up her body, covering her in heavy paint. When he came eye level with her breasts, his face mere inches away, she trembled. If only it was Danny within kissing distance of her nipples. But Danny was over in Iraq. If he were here, she'd never have the nerve to go through with this, even wearing a mask.

"Why is such a lovely woman so nervous? You should be proud to display such a beautiful body," he said as he sprayed white paint over half of each nipple.

"You're not going to leave them exposed are you?" Scandalized but thrilled, her nipples pebbled.

The man laughed. "*Oui, mon cheri.* I should, they are so beautiful, but I will cover them half in black if you insist."

"Only cover one completely." Tia, the brazen hussy, winked at her.

Heat suffused Paige's chest and traveled into her cheeks. "No! Cover both completely or I'll wash it off now." She felt like she was holding his painting hostage, which, in effect, she was.

"But it's so very beautiful this way." The man sighed deeply and held up the airbrush. "If you insist, but it is against my artistic judgment."

"Don't!" Tia rushed over and held her hand in front of the airbrush. "It's so scintillating this way. At least let him finish the rest of you and view the finished product before you make up your mind."

Half an hour later, when the paint had dried, masks were securely in place, Paige and Tia ventured outside. A gentle breeze caressed their bodies and Paige's nipples puckered.

She scanned the crowded streets for signs of policeman. To her horror, most of the other women were merely topless, not completely nude. Shorts covered their pussies. At least G-strings. "We're going to jail."

Tia growled. "Chill. No one's going to jail and we're not going to burn in hell. See?" She pointed to a pair of policemen dining at an outdoor café. "They're enjoying the view. They never bother anybody long as you keep the peace."

"Nice costumes," a young man said in a western drawl.

Tia swiped the air with her paw and then squealed and hugged him. "Leo! Is it really you?"

"In the flesh, darlin'."

Paige froze and almost fell flat on her face. *Leo? The Leo, Danny's buddy?*

"We're home." More squealing ensued, and then loud smooching.

Paige's heart stopped as ice formed in her veins. "*We?*" She managed to squeak out, her vision blurry, her world rocking.

Leo broke his kiss to smile wickedly at her. "Yep. You heard me right. Turn around."

Wildfire licked her twitching pussy and her nipples contracted. She should have made François cover it fully instead of letting it peek out! This is how she was going to be reunited with Danny?

Tia was so dead. She had known the guys would be here and tricked her into coming and getting naked. She mouthed to her ex-best friend, "I'll get you for this!"

The incorrigible slut merely laughed merrily before resuming her tongue-wrestling match with her soldier.

"Aren't you going to welcome me home? I had hoped for something more like he's getting, not the cold shoulder."

Warm hands fell on her shoulders and then gently turned her around. "Wow!" Danny's appreciative eyes roamed over her breasts and then down to her pussy where they remained several long moments, stoking her fire.

She swallowed hard as she allowed him to hold her hands. Licking her lips, she asked, "Nice costume, huh?"

Such a scintillating welcome home. Next semester she needed to enroll in Conversation 101.

"Looks like I owe you a mess of kisses." He pulled her into his arms, against his strongly beating heart, snuggled against his burgeoning erection.

"Tons," she said, lifting her lips to collect the overdue kisses. If only he would lose the uniform so she could mold her naked flesh to his.

"Uhm." Danny captured her lips in a searing kiss as he touched her half-visible nipple with his fingers. Against her lips, he mumbled, "I never imagined a homecoming like this."

Nor had she in her wildest dreams. She prayed she wouldn't awake to find it was all just a dream. "Did you know you were meeting us here?" She looked down at herself. "Like this?"

Danny chuckled. "No. It seems we have two conniving best friends."

She glanced at the schemers and gasped. Tia had her arms and legs wrapped around her soldier and the pair of policemen were frowning at them and rising from their table.

"Uh-oh. Parading naked in costume may be okay but making love in the street obviously isn't." Her stomach clenched as she stepped back from Danny.

He caught her hand preventing her complete flight. Then he dragged her over to their friends and tapped Leo's shoulder. "Come on, bubba, before we get free lodging in separate male/female quarters. Let's take this party back to our room — in private."

Paige blinked several times, her fluttering lashes tickling her cheeks. Her words stuck in her throat. They were going to continue this in private? Just how much continuance?

Leo moaned in protest. "Can't a man have any fun?"

"In private," Danny growled, tugging her forcefully behind him. Either he really didn't want to be locked up or he really wanted to get her alone.

Juice flowed hot and heavy from her pussy at the thought. Danny couldn't wait to fuck her. She couldn't wait to open her legs wide and feel his possession. She prayed she didn't misread him. If so, she'd just have to seduce him. But if this ultimate seductress's outfit didn't work, nothing would.

A seeming eternity later, Danny unlocked a hotel door and escorted her across the threshold of a room with two queen-sized beds. Leo and Tia followed, kissing and petting heavily. Tia's paint was smeared so that her lioness costume was almost unrecognizable.

The other couple fell onto the closest bed as together they ripped off Leo's clothing.

She was in the Twilight Zone! No way was Leo going to fuck Tia in front of them. Tia was brave but not that brave—was she?

Fascinated, she couldn't tear her gaze from the other couple as her friend climbed on top the naked very well endowed soldier and slid down his swollen cock.

Paige cleared her throat, her pussy quivering, and her nerves tingling. "Shouldn't we go somewhere else where we can talk? And let them have some privacy?" Not that it seemed to matter to Leo or Tia.

When she tried to duck under Danny's arm to escape, he blocked her way and locked the door. He backed her up against it and leaned over her, his mesmerizing lips mere fractions of an inch from hers. "I couldn't small talk now if our lives depended on it. Don't you know how hot and horny your letters have made me? I promised you a passel of kisses and you're going to get them, right here, right now. An officer and a gentleman always keeps his word."

Her gaze fell to the flexing bulge in his slacks and she licked her suddenly parched lips. Fear and excitement thrummed through her veins. They were really going to make love. She covered his hand in hers and tugged. "Let's go to my room."

A sexy devilish grin stole over Danny's handsomely rugged features. "You scared to be in the same room with them?"

Caught. She shook her head as Tia screamed in ecstasy and Leo grunted his supreme satisfaction. "Terrified."

Danny leaned closer and teased her lips with his. His rough shirt grazed her nipples and she groaned. "I make love to you in all my dreams. Now you're finally here, I can't wait another minute to fuck you." He plundered her lips with masterful kisses that spun her world upside down.

Gently, he drew her over to the far bed where she lay down and gazed up at him with love. He towered over her, gazing upon her with passion-glazed eyes as he tore off his offending clothes.

She gasped in admiration and desire when his full, velvety cock sprang out of his pants and pointed at her pussy. Wet and glossy, it was ready to take possession. If things got any better, she might have to hire someone to help her enjoy it.

When he lowered his pants, she gasped when she spied a long, puckered scar on his leg. Reaching out, she ran her fingertip down its length. "Did this happen in the war?"

Grimacing, Danny glanced down at his leg. "It looks worse than it is. It's healing or they'd have put me out of the Air Force."

Relief flooded Paige. Of course he wouldn't still be in the Air Force if he were injured too badly. Or at least he'd be in a medical facility, not traipsing about Key West. "Does it hurt?"

"Just a little twinge every now and then. Don't worry. It won't affect me making wild, passionate love to you," he drawled.

As he lowered himself over her, putting his weight on his bulging arms, she said in all fairness, "You only owe me kisses."

A guttural growl arose from his throat. "Make love to me, woman."

At the last second, sanity returned. "I'm not on birth control. Do you have any protection?" Not that she wouldn't love Danny's seed to fill her, but he had only professed his desire to make love, not to love her forever. And she had almost a year 'til she finished her master's.

Her soldier grimaced but rolled off. He opened the nightstand drawer, which was overflowing with condoms of all colors, styles and flavors.

"I thought you said you didn't know I was here."

"Leo did." Danny selected a red, white and blue patriotic condom and handed it to her. "Put it on me, babe," he said in a husky voice as he gazed deeply into her eyes. He ripped the foil package open with his teeth and handed it to her. Without warning, he suckled a pert nipple, pulling it deeply into his mouth.

His tongue flicked over it and then he nibbled gently making her writhe beneath him.

"More of that and I'll never get this on." She encircled his beautiful shaft with one hand and slid it up to find the satiny, slick tip. She slid the latex over it and gently worked it down as he suckled her nipple more fiercely.

Danny burrowed between her thighs, spread them wide and then thrust into her strong and deep. Her cries of ecstasy matched Tia's as she lifted her hips and met him thrust for thrust.

His strong hands kneaded her breasts as he stroked against her pussy, enflaming her.

On fire, she ran her hands down every inch of his finely honed body, in awe that he was hers, even for one night.

Out of breath, they panted, their tongues mating as, a few feet away on the neighboring bed, Tia screamed and flung herself over Leo.

It was so incredibly erotic to make love with the other couple in the room that she was carried away on the wings of emotion and climaxed several times as Danny plunged his length to the hilt.

When the rapturous waves subsided so that she could breathe normally, Danny licked and suckled her nipples restoking her fire. In absolute rapture, she moaned as Leo and Tia watched with heavy-lidded sex-drenched expressions.

Danny lay on his back and held out his arms to her. "Come here." He flexed his cock and his eyebrows. "Ride me, darlin'."

Her pussy clenched and she nodded eagerly as she straddled him. In a teasing mood, she hovered over his cock, rubbing her pussy over the tip.

He growled, encircled her waist with his large, calloused hands and helped her slide down his incredible length. Ravenous for his hot, delicious cock, she rode him hard as he bucked beneath her.

Leaning forward, his abs straining, Danny nibbled her nipple, then pulled it into his mouth, nearly sending her over the edge. He was so impossibly deep, so lusciously hot, she voted they stay in bed fucking forever.

"You taste so good, babe. Better than licorice," Danny mumbled around her tit.

She writhed happily at his high praise and cradled his head to her chest. Letting her fingers run through his clipped hair, she wished the military would let it grow out so she could bury her face in its pre-military silkiness.

She hadn't noticed that Leo had risen from his bed until another set of hands encircled her waist, sending electric jolts through her. "May I join in?"

Umm. She had always longed to be fucked by two men at once, but never dreamed they would be such incredible hotties. When the tip of Leo's hot slick cock rubbed down the crack of her buttocks, she jumped. This couldn't be happening. She glanced quickly at her friend to make sure she was okay.

Tia grinned broadly and stretched out languidly on the bed, stroking her finger in and out of her pussy. "Go for it, sweetie, but share alike."

Festival fever engulfing her, every inch of her tingling with anticipation, she tilted her head, giving Leo full access to the long column of her throat. To have two cocks deep inside her, two sets of lips cherishing her feverish flesh, flooding her with unimaginable ecstasy…pleasuring her…pure nirvana.

Her breathing ragged, she looked to Danny, fearing he would be jealous or angry, but willing him to be open-minded and generous. She was so hot for two cocks at once that she squirmed, grinding her hips to Danny's.

"The idea makes you hot, doesn't it, babe? He can fuck your back hole but I'm the only one allowed to fuck your pussy. That's all mine." Danny stroked her mons with his hand and massaged her clit with his thumb as he gazed up at her with a smoldering passion that made her pussy clench around his cock.

Thrills shooting through her, she nodded as Leo donned a new condom and climbed onto the bed behind her. "Yes! Fuck my brains out!"

Leo's arms curled around her and he played with her breasts for several minutes while he licked her neck. Then he teased her buttocks with his hot shaft, before finally inserting the head. When she thought she would die of frustration and longing, Leo plunged his cock impossibly deep. God, it was so tight and delectable as it rammed in and out in rhythm with Danny's cock, which claimed her pussy.

Two hot hands stroked her pussy while a hand massaged and kneaded each breast.

Leo lathered the back of her neck with his tongue as she writhed against the two beautiful men.

A huge mass of sensation, she clenched the two huge dicks inside her greedily, never wanting to set either free. She could die happy with these two amazing cocks fucking her senseless. Every woman should have two gorgeous hunks worshipping her body such. Then there would truly be peace in the world forever more. Everybody would be too busy making love to make war. She seriously considered suggesting it as a peacekeeping measure to the United Nations.

"You're wonderful, babe." Danny gazed up at her with adoration as he continued to massage her clit and Leo bathed her ear with his tongue.

"You're both so very incredible," she managed to rasp as fireworks exploded deep inside. The men thrust deeper and faster. They held her captive until they'd brought her to climax three more magnificent times.

"I've never come so much. I didn't know I could." She gazed lovingly at her Danny and clenched her vagina around his beloved cock. Hugging him, she brushed her lips over his and mumbled, "Thank you."

Leo pulled out slowly so that only Danny's cock remained inside. The cowboy returned to Tia and kissed her deeply as Danny drank deeply of her lips. "I'm afraid we ruined your costume. I'll buy you a new one."

"You don't have to." She snuggled deeply into his arms and laid her ear against his rapidly beating heart. If she was truly naked, she couldn't go outside and she'd have to stay in Danny's bed, naked, forever. She tingled all over at the thought and licked Danny's nipple, making him writhe. She could stand to be in Danny's bed for an eternity. "You've worn me out."

"I'm not," Tia said in a sultry tone. "I'm ready for some of what you got."

She wiggled her finger at Danny. "You, stud, take your place."

Danny kissed Paige tenderly on the lips. "You don't mind?"

Paige shook her head. "As long as you don't fuck her pussy. Your cock belongs in my pussy only."

"Agreed. Get some rest. You'll need it. I'm going to connect the dots when I get back."

She quivered deliciously in anticipation. "Go ahead. I'll watch."

Danny strolled over to her friend, his gorgeous cock swelling again. Excitement blazed in his eyes as he crawled onto the bed with Leo and Tia and took one of her nipples into his mouth and kneaded the other with his hand. Moaning, he kissed his way over to its twin, and bathed it with his tongue. More paint wiped onto Danny's face so that he, too, started to resemble a tiger.

"She has sweet tits, doesn't she?" Leo beamed proudly as he drilled her.

"Umm." Danny kissed and nibbled his way around Tia, holding onto her breasts, rubbing her nipples between his fingers.

"You have magical lips, stud. No wonder Paige can't get enough of you." Tia batted her lashes at Danny. "What are you waiting for? Don't you want to rock and roll with us?"

Danny rose to his knees behind Tia's lush bottom and rubbed his glistening cock over her buttocks.

"Tease," Tia accused, wiggling her butt in his face. "I don't know how much longer I can be patient for my turn. Give me some of that hot cock."

With a growl rumbling in his chest, Danny rolled on a new latex condom and then plunged into her. He put his hands around her waist and rammed full-hilt into her, until Tia screamed with ecstasy. "Oh yes!"

Paige had expected to be flooded with jealousy at the sight of her man screwing another woman, especially her best friend, but she wasn't. Instead, she was majorly turned on and her own juices flowed uncontrollably as his delicious cock rammed in and out so masterfully. He was all man—macho, fierce and brimming over with testosterone. He had the sexiest, most impressive cock she'd ever seen, so velvety, so red it was almost crimson, so hard and amazingly long.

When Tia moaned and writhed, so did she. She kneaded her nipple with one hand and stroked her finger in and out of her cunt with the other as Danny watched her lovingly.

The men brought Tia to climax several times until she pleaded for mercy and Danny finally pulled his magnificent cock out and brought it home to her.

She opened her arms wide to him, shivering. "Welcome home, soldier. Fuck me again." She was so hot for her man she couldn't stand another moment without his cock pumping her. Spreading her legs wide, she chafed as he put on a new condom.

"It's cherry flavored," he whispered suggestively, making her mouth water.

"How come we never did this before you left for Iraq?" She encircled his cock with her hand and tugged it gently to her pussy.

"I didn't know you wanted me to. " Something indiscernible flickered across his eyes and she wished she could read his mind.

She lifted her hips to his, aching for his cock to fill her again, her vagina clenching. "I've loved you since I met you."

Danny froze. "You *love* me?" He rolled off her and stood next to the bed, raking unsteady fingers through his hair. Pure, unadulterated fright flashed across his eyes. "Whoa. That's quite an honor. And a responsibility."

He didn't sound as if it was an honor. Quite the opposite.

Paige stared at the alien hovering above her wondering where her Danny had gone, or if he'd ever truly been here. The word 'love' clearly frightened him. She could smell his fear.

So he wasn't in love with her and she was a burden. She should have known the moment he let Leo fuck her and especially when he'd fucked Tia. Acid tears stung the backs of her eyes and she blinked them back furiously. "Forget I said anything. I got swept away in the moment."

Furious at her foolish self, she wrapped the sheet about her, toga style, and left quickly, deafening herself to Danny's insincere protests. She wished she'd never heard of Fantasy Fest and especially not that conniving rascal Danny Napolitano.

Devastated, she ran for the elevator and it closed in Danny's face.

* * * * *

Damn! He'd just won the ass of the year award— twice. First he'd fucked her friend and then froze when she professed love for him.

She'd noticed the scar and hadn't she noticed him limping? That he wasn't a complete man and might never be again? He couldn't give himself to her as only half a man. He wouldn't know 'til after his next surgery if he'd be complete again. It could take several surgeries. Maybe a lifetime of surgeries.

Damn Leo and Tia for putting them in this position and complicating the hell out of an already extremely messy situation!

He tried to run down the stairs after Paige, but stumbled and fell down half a flight. Moaning in excruciating pain, he held his leg. *Damn damn damn!* A complete man wouldn't let his woman run away hurt and angry. No matter how he tried, he couldn't stand or even drag himself up or down the stairs.

Swallowing his pride, he yelled for help, hoping some old lady didn't come to his rescue and find him in all his glory. Perhaps if he hadn't spent his energy screwing her friend, he wouldn't have fallen.

It was for the best. Let her believe him a cad. He was, after all. A real man wouldn't have to prove himself macho by fucking two women, one of them his woman's best friend. It had meant nothing. Just Festival fever. More in the way of proof he was still a man. He knew Paige's rose-tinted feelings would overlook his disability but he had worried he couldn't please a woman not already enchanted with him.

So he'd proved himself still virile and less a man in the eyes of the woman he loved. *Idiot! Bastard!*

He wasn't good enough for her now, but he hadn't wanted to hurt her either.

He worried for her safety alone and naked in the wild Festival streets. And it was all his fault. Some man he was.

Finally Leo and Tia found him. He could barely stand to gaze upon his former sex partner. That's all it had been was sex.

"We're taking you to the hospital." Leo hoisted him in his arms and carried him back to their room, while Tia held doors wide.

"No. Find Paige. She's alone out there." Danny gritted his teeth against the sizzling pain.

"Can you blame her?" Tia faced off against Danny, anger sparkling in her eyes, her hand on her hip. She wore

Leo's shirt, which barely fell to the tops of her thighs. "She tells you she loves you and you say, '*Whoa*'? Some officer and gentleman you are."

Leo whirled on her. "Back off. You don't know everything. He's got enough to handle."

"I'm not a mind reader." Tia waited for a few moments in silence, her brow arched. "Well?"

"It's up to Dan whether or not he wants to tell you." Leo dropped a supportive hand on Danny's shoulder.

Danny shook his head and pursed his lips. He didn't want Paige to know about his impending dangerous surgery. If Tia knew, she'd tell Paige.

"Fine! You make quite a pair. I just hope she'll talk to me." Tia slammed out the door, making the men wince.

Chapter Seven

Despite his protests, Leo had Danny carted off to the nearest hospital, which proceeded to ship him to the medical facility at Keesler Air Force Base. Leo had accompanied him while Tia went in search of Paige.

"We're going to take you into surgery now, Captain. We've notified your commanding officer but, if there's any family you would like to inform, we can help you do so." The lanky civilian doctor soothed him a small measure with his calm demeanor.

Danny crossed his arms over his chest and strengthened his flagging resolve. "Just my folks. There's no need to be worrying them."

"You'll need a support system, son. You may be laid up for several months and you're going to need physical therapy afterward." The doctor regarded him quizzically over the top of his wire-rimmed spectacles and clucked his tongue. "There's nothing to be ashamed of."

He scowled at his disturbing thoughts. Good thing the man didn't know the whole story of how he came to take a tumble down the stairs and do further damage to his already injured leg.

Leo cleared his throat and stepped closer to his hospital bed. "You should let Paige know."

Danny growled at his partner in crime. "She's the last one I want knowing." At the glint in his friend's eyes, he added, "And don't you be telling her."

"My hunch is she'd be more understanding and forgiving if she knew." Leo lowered his voice to barely above a whisper so that Danny had to strain to catch his words. "You owe her that much."

The doctor's fatherly look pierced him. "We can't force you to tell your loved ones but we highly advise it. In my experience, they prefer to know beforehand rather than after the fact. The nurse will be in shortly to prep you for surgery." He moved discreetly onto his next patient with a shake of his salt-and-pepper head.

"If you hadn't dragged me here under false pretenses and then started that gang bang..." Danny felt like decking his lieutenant and would have if he could get out of this freakin' bed. Then he sunk deep into his pillows, the fight seeping out of him as he accepted his share of the responsibility. "If I hadn't gotten carried away and wanted to prove I was Macho Man..."

Leo laid a commiserative hand on Danny's shoulder and squeezed. "From where I was standing, she was as much a willing participant as you, so I wouldn't horsewhip myself about it."

True. Paige had appeared to enjoy the fun more than he had. Perhaps he should be the angry one. The vivid picture of his buddy fucking his woman flashed back to him and a string of curses tumbled off his lips. Normally he wouldn't stand for another man touching his woman's hand, much less give him permission to screw her. But they'd all been carried away by Festival fever and out of their minds with lust. He and Leo saw it as just sex, but would Paige, participant or not? Women had funny notions about this love-sex business and had trouble separating them for what they really were.

A no-nonsense civilian nurse pushed an IV into the room. She gave the evil eye to Leo as she bustled around Danny. "Visiting hours are over, young man. Your friend needs his rest."

Leo screwed up his lips. "See you later, sleeping beauty. Don't go stirring up no more hornets' nests."

* * * * *

Paige showered, trying to wash Danny from her soul. Then she hurriedly dressed and caught a cab to the airport, perversely glad that no one had stopped her, and disgruntled that Danny hadn't tried to follow her.

Responsibility!

So that's how he viewed her. All this time he had only been playing with her, using her to get through a rough situation. Worse, she had suspected this could be the case and she'd still let herself fall desperately in love with him.

Tonight had been thrilling at first, when she'd been lost in magical, larger-than-life sensations. She'd ridden to the zenith of the mountain just to be cruelly hurled into the bubbling volcano of despair.

Despair? She snorted as she plunked down her return ticket in hopes of exchanging it for an earlier flight. What was there to despair about? A pen pal relationship that fell short of her unrealistic expectations?

Her first clue should have been that Danny hadn't sought her out or even told her he was returning home. It was Leo who had sought Tia out. She and Danny had just been dragged along for the ride.

She grimaced at her bad analogy. What a ride it had been. One she'd never forget. Also one she'd never repeat.

"I'm afraid there are no flights available today. I can put your name on the stand-by list in case of a cancellation," the young flight attendant said with a sparkling smile.

Paige swallowed a sigh and nodded. "Put me on the list." She would have thought Festival-goers would still be arriving in droves, not departing. Perhaps others had found Festival as disenchanting as she had.

Finally, there was a cancellation that evening that took her to Atlanta, where she transferred to Jackson, Mississippi. If Danny had really wanted to find her, he'd had plenty of time in the fourteen hours she had been waiting. Obviously, he wasn't interested in catching up with her. She would have thought the airport was the obvious place to look.

* * * * *

Danny awoke from surgery slowly, a heavy mist fogging his vision, his throat dry and sore, his thoughts jumbled. He blinked rapidly, his eyes unfocused. "Water."

Where was he? His thick tongue refused to work the syllables properly and his voice sounded muted and groggy.

An angel in white floated to him. "You're at Keesler Air Force Base Hospital and you just had surgery on your leg."

He was in Mississippi? He narrowed his eyes, straining to clear his vision and the pea soup in his head. Her pristine white uniform adorned by the double silver bars of a captain became clear, as did his memory.

"Paige," he mumbled, struggling to sit up. He had to find her.

The captain held him down. "You won't be able to walk on that leg for a while. Just relax and we'll return you to your room shortly."

She offered him a miniscule medicine cup's worth of water. It was barely a drop on his parched tongue.

He chafed as he fell in and out of consciousness. He swore at his predicament. He wanted to find Paige and ensure her safety, but he didn't want her to see him emasculated this way. He didn't want her pity and he was afraid that's what it would be if she were to see him in this condition. He couldn't bear that.

He wondered how long this would delay his separation from the army. He had been due to muster out in a few days. He'd scheduled an appointment to speak to his ex-employer about getting his job back. It looked like his life was on indefinite hold. He feared he might get to know the VA hospitals very well and spend his days there like so many of the old Vietnam vets, a prospect he did not relish.

He supposed he should be thankful he had made it home alive but he felt none too grateful. Just the opposite. He could be crippled for life and that's exactly why he couldn't have a future with Paige. It wouldn't be fair to saddle her with half a man.

Knowing her so well, he was sure her high sense of honor would propel her to support him, even marry him whether she loved him or not. Eventually, she would come to regret her decision and resent him. She'd long for a complete, real man and he wouldn't be able to satisfy her. He'd had a taste of her ravenous sexual appetite and only a virile man would do.

So he wouldn't prolong the torture for either of them and would cut ties here. Better she hate him, thinking he was a no-good bastard, than pour out her pity on him just to think him a pathetic wimp in the end.

The true blue buddy he was, Leo awaited him when he was wheeled into his room three hours later. The soldier tried to erase the worry lines creasing his forehead before Danny saw them but he was too astute. He pretended not to see them, however. When the orderlies lifted him from the stretcher and shifted him to the bed, he had to bite back a growl at his own inability to perform such a simple task for himself.

After the staff stopped fussing over him and ensured his IV drip was secure, they left them in peace.

Leo hunkered down beside him, his expression surly. "You sure you don't want Paige to know where you are?"

Danny bolted up in the bed, instantly regretting the impulsive move when his thigh throbbed. Gritting his teeth against the pain, he asked sharply, "Does that mean you found her?"

Leo's gaze shifted uneasily away and he cleared his throat. "No. Uh. At least Tia's not called me if she has. Of course my phone's off so she can't reach me."

He waved the cell phone in the air. "I should go call her and see."

Danny nodded, exhaustion seeping into his bones. He suspected the nurse had put some sleeping aid into his IV solution. "Do that. But don't tell Paige about this."

Uncertainty flashed across his friend's eyes, alarming him.

He caught his wrist in an iron grip. "I mean it, bubba. Swear to me right now that you will not tell her and that you will swear Tia to secrecy, too."

Leo flinched. "I swear I won't say a word but Tia's a law unto herself."

"Like you said, Paige has been hurt enough." He sunk heavily into his pillows, his energy waning.

"I didn't mean it that way..." Leo stammered, raking unsteady fingers through his unruly hair.

"Do it!" Danny growled, his lids too heavy to prop open any longer. As darkness claimed him, the pain faded in blessed relief.

Chapter Eight

Late and breathless from sprinting across campus, Paige rushed into the computer store. When Paul glared at her, she smiled her apologies. "I was waylaid by my professor. Sorry."

"We need to talk," Paul said, his voice devoid of emotion. "Follow me."

"I'll just put my books down back here..."

"Bring them with you." His voice couldn't be icier nor could his back be any straighter.

She gulped, not liking his demeanor one bit. What had she done to deserve such chilliness? He led her to his boss's office where not only his superior, the head of the book store, but the head campus accountant, the internal auditor and a policeman awaited them.

Lucy, the auditor, stood. "Come in and close the door."

Paul nodded and motioned to Paige to take the hot seat in the center of the room. "These folks have some questions for you."

Lucy smiled at him and took center stage, towering over her, the policeman standing rigid behind her. "Petty cash has systematically been missing from the computer store."

Paige's throat went dry. She was one of the few primarily responsible for counting and safeguarding the petty cash.

Lucy continued. "You signed off on the books every time there was a shortage."

Stunned, bile rising in her throat, Paige rose from her chair, protesting. "Are you accusing me of theft? I didn't take one cent." Still, guilt assaulted her as she recalled a few times she couldn't balance the books and had put it down to her ineptitude. She should have alerted Paul immediately. Some accountant she was. As of this minute, she was definitely changing her major, not wishing to be responsible for anyone else's money ever again. That's if they didn't kick her out of school—or throw her in jail.

Paul's boss stood, her arms folded across her flat chest, her eyes mere chips of ice. "We're not accusing you...yet. But we'd like to hear an explanation of the shortages if you can offer any."

Paige sank back in her chair, racking her brain for the correct accounting terminology. "I had noticed once or twice that there was a small discrepancy but when I looked the next day, everything balanced so I thought it was just my error."

Lucy asked, "And you didn't tell your boss or his boss?" Sunlight glinted off her glossy locks, highlighting the spun gold strands.

Paige swallowed hard. "No, like I said earlier. Everything always balanced the next day. I'm new to the job so I'm just learning and I get confused sometimes."

A sigh escaped Paul's lips. "You should have let me know if you had such difficulty. Perhaps this wasn't the job for you."

Paige sank into a quagmire of self-doubt. Accounting definitely wasn't the job for her. But what was? The only thing she hadn't wrecked of late was losing weight and Tia had coached her with that. "I suppose not," she mumbled, clasping her books tightly.

"As of this moment, you are officially suspended from your job pending the outcome of this investigation," Paul's boss said, looking down her long, skinny nose at Paige. "You are not to step foot in the computer store. We will be in contact with you when the investigation is concluded or if we have additional questions."

When the policeman stepped forward, Paige sucked in her breath. "Miss Forbes, I must advise you not to leave town, and not to contact any of your former co-workers."

This sounded very serious. "Am I suspended from school?"

Lucy regarded her quizzically. "No. Not yet."

Not yet resonated in Paige's brain. They wanted to expel and jail her! Was it merely mismanagement or had someone been stealing from the store? Who would steal? Why? And why did all the signs presumably only point to her?

She pierced the auditor with her stare. "Are there any other suspects? I'm not the only one responsible for the petty cash."

Lucy leaned back against the desk and crossed her ankles. "I'm not at liberty to say. I can only say that the investigation is ongoing."

Paul whispered something to Lucy who shook her head. Then she said, "We feel that we must let you go from your employment in any case, as you failed to report the continuing discrepancies."

Devastated, her stomach lurched. "Am I eligible for other campus employment? I mean, where money isn't involved?"

"I'm afraid not until this matter is closed and then depending on the final outcome."

Of course this black mark would be on her record making it difficult or impossible to obtain other employment. Who wanted to hire a suspected thief? Or an inept accountant? Not that she would ever touch someone else's money again even though that severely limited her selection of part-time employment, especially in a small college town over two hours from any major cities.

Maybe she should change colleges, start all over. New town. New campus. New major. Nothing was left for her here.

Except that she wasn't allowed to leave town by order of the police. Also if she dropped out mid-semester, she'd fail the semester. It was too late to withdraw.

What graduate school would allow a suspected thief to enroll? Maybe she should forget college and join the army now that she fell within their allowable weight limits. Hadn't she considered enlisting before when she didn't meet the minimum requirements? If not for the possibility of running into Danny or Leo, the idea held merit.

"Is that all? May I go now?" How could Paul believe this of her? They had been friends. At least she had thought so.

"I'll escort you out." Grim-faced, Paul crossed the room and held the door for her.

Lifting her chin high, she said, "Thank you but I know my way out." She sailed past him not wishing to see him ever again.

Paul followed her. "You don't understand. I have to make sure you leave the premises."

Bless his soul. Rub salt in her raw wounds. She sent him a withering look. "What? The entire Student Union is off limits to me? I have a PO Box here. I have to buy supplies for my classes."

Her former boss stopped and chewed his lower lip. "Don't step foot in the computer store and don't hang about out front." With that, he stood guard in front of his store when they reached it.

Like she wanted to see the lousy store or him ever again? Seething, she visited her favorite ice cream parlor and ordered a jumbo banana split.

After she'd indulged in two large scrumptious spoonfuls, she heard a familiar voice. "I thought I'd find you here."

Her gut clenching, Paige almost dropped the spoon. Guilty of at least cheating on her diet, if not on the books, Paige lifted her gaze to meet Tia's as the woman invited herself to sit at the table.

"Why'd you run off that way? We've all been worried sick. And just what do you think you're doing? That thing has more calories than you're allowed to eat for three days!" Tia treated her to the motherly stare she so detested and snatched the utensil from her hand, looking at it as if it was a monster.

Drowning herself in her sorrows.

Paige snatched it back and delved deeply into the creamy concoction with relish. She was so sick of counting calories. So sick of being accused of something. "Eating, if you don't mind."

Incorrigible, Tia grabbed it again and held it hostage. "You don't know the whole story. Danny has his reasons."

Paige digested this news. She leaned back in her chair and crossed her arms over her chest with a deep sigh. "And I suppose you know his big secret?"

Tia's gaze flickered away from hers uneasily and she gave an almost imperceptible nod of her head.

Paige waited several seconds for a reply. When none seemed forthcoming, she asked, "Well? You said if I knew, I'd be more understanding. So tell me."

Tia sucked in a deep breath and met her gaze squarely. "I can't. They've sworn me to secrecy."

Paige stared at the brunette, wondering if she heard right. *What kind of head games were they playing with her?* "Sooooo. I should know but you can't help me? But you're letting me know that I'm not allowed to know so I can fret over some big secret?" The logic eluded her.

She hazarded a guess. "I suppose you want me to forgive him?" She looked around pointedly. "Where is he? Funny. I don't see him here. He doesn't seem anxious to talk to me."

"He'd be here if he could." Tia looked absolutely miserable, almost as miserable as she felt, all gray and cloudy and storm-tossed. Then fear squeezed her heart as a horrid thought struck her. "Was he sent back to Iraq?" She held her breath and her heart skipped several beats.

"No. He's still in the States."

"But he doesn't want to see me." *That made just about everybody.*

"It's not like that…"

"But you won't tell me. He doesn't want me to know." Still royally bitter, she scraped her chair back and stood to leave. She hitched her purse over her shoulder and pivoted on her heel without a goodbye.

Footsteps rushed up behind her and then Tia was at her side. "I'm sure he'll tell you in his time. Don't be mad at me."

"I'm mad at the world," Paige mumbled under her breath.

"Just because Danny didn't profess his undying love for you in an awkward moment? It takes men a while to admit their true feelings."

Paige paused and closed her eyes. "It's not only that."

"What else has happened?"

Paige wasn't of a mind to bare her soul to Tia when the woman was keeping her lips so tightly shut, that she kept mum and walked on.

"I would tell you if I could. It's not my secret to tell."

It hurt that Tia knew Danny's secrets and she didn't. What didn't he want her to know? What could be so terrible? More likely he didn't want her involved in his life.

"I'm not leaving 'til you tell me what's eating you." Tia's shadow mingled with Paige's under the late afternoon Mississippi sun.

"Fine." Her nostrils flaring, Paige stopped dead on the sidewalk across from the university. "I've been accused of theft and canned from my job. You happy?"

A couple of passersby shot odd looks her way.

"That's awful! You aren't a crook." Tia's features screwed up in anger. "What idiot accused you of thievery?"

She held up her fingers and ticked them off. "The internal auditor, my boss, his boss and the campus controller." She didn't add the uniformed policeman to her verbal list.

Her friend's jaw dropped and she shook her head furiously so that her raven locks slapped her cheeks. "Then you've been framed." Tia narrowed her eyes so that they were mere slits. "Who else handles the money?"

"Only the four of us and Paul. Benny, Kristen, Penny and me."

Fire flashed in Tia's charcoal eyes and she clenched her hands. "That witch!"

Paige regarded her skeptically waiting for the revelation.

"Penny! You see how strange she's been acting. How she's been flaunting her expensive new clothes all the while she's moaning how poor she is. She doesn't have a sugar daddy. She's a thief!"

Paige's jaw dropped and her heart raced. *It fit!* "We have the same initials — *PF*. It would be so easy for her."

"Then she should be under suspicion, too." Paige twisted her lips. "Yeah, she should be."

She whirled on her friend and made her swear. "Not a word to Danny or Leo."

"But…"

"I don't want Danny knowing anything about this." He'd forfeited the right, not that he seemed to care. "Swear you won't tell either of them."

Tia glowered at her. "I swear. The two of you will be the death of me."

Bless her heart, it was the least she deserved for setting up that fiasco in Key West. "You'll live."

When Paige arrived home, the police awaited her with a warrant to search her room. The dorm mother tried to keep the other students back, but Merline elbowed her way to the front, scowling the entire way.

"What in the blue blazes is going on?" Merline asked, hissing, her normally placid blue eyes ablaze with outrage. "What have you done?"

Mortified, Paige whispered back, "Nothing. I'll fill you in later."

"You've should've filled me in before they cordoned off my room! I can't even get to my books and I have a big project due tomorrow!"

"Miss Forbes," A middle-aged Cajun policeman said, "Please stand over there, miss, and do not converse with anyone."

Merline spun on her heel and marched off, brimming with self-righteous indignation.

Lordy! She had trouble in spades and she hadn't done a single thing to deserve it. Her cell phone rang and the display read out Tia's name. She flipped it open and whispered in hushed tones, "I can't talk right now. I'll call you later." At least she hoped she could.

Officer Boudreaux confiscated her phone. "We'll return it later," he had promised and then took down the phone number and wireless company information.

She wondered when the reporters would be by to try and hang her on national television. She seethed with fury, wanting to choke the true culprit for setting her up and her boss for believing the worst about her. God forgive her, but she didn't see the humor in the situation. Someone was out to fry her and ruin her good name. She'd be lucky to get a job in sanitary engineering after this.

She rued while the cops tore apart her room and pawed through her personal items. Merline would never forgive her and she couldn't totally blame her.

An eternity later, they carted away her personal records for closer inspection. They might as well have thrown her in the pokey and melted the key for they had already tried and convicted her in their minds. Sentencing seemed all that remained.

How long was the prison term for embezzlement? Judging by their attitudes, it would be a good many years. The fresh bloom of youth would be long gone from her cheeks before they released her back into society.

She needed an attorney.

Her stomach tied in knots, she couldn't eat the rest of the day. Restless, she ambled around Hattiesburg on foot, avoiding the campus where suspicious stares bored into her.

When her tired feet carried her home, she found Tia camped out in front of her room. Her friend expelled a long yawn and rose to her feet, stretching. "Where in the dickens have you been all day? What's going on now?"

"Here and there." She couldn't rightly remember where she'd been. Everything was a blur. She'd never before been on half the roads she'd wandered down today. Hattiesburg now seemed a much larger place than she had previously imagined.

With a sigh, she unlocked her door and came face-to-face with a furious roommate.

"Oh no you don't, missy. You just waltz your fanny right back out of this room. Those strong-armed thugs went through my drawers and turned everything upside down." Anger smoldered in Merline's hateful glare.

Paige repressed a moan. Was this how the rest of her life was going to play out? Everyone would convict and reject her without a trial? "I'm innocent. I've not done anything wrong."

Merline cut her off and thrust a large box at her, revulsion flashing through her eyes. "They say you've been stealing from your job. Have you been stealing from me, too? Is that why I've come up short a few times this month? I bet you skimmed off the top of that soldiers' fund of yours, too."

Aghast, Paige sucked in a sharp breath. "I'm not a thief and I've not stolen a thing from you or anybody else."

"How'd you afford to go to the Keys? You keep bemoaning how poor you are. I know how you paid for it. With my money, the soldiers' and the university's."

Bristling, Tia stepped forward. "I paid for her trip. It was a gift."

"Whatevah," Merline drawled and tried to slam the door in her face.

Paige blocked it. "I beg your pardon but I take offense to being accused of stealing and not being let in my own room."

Merline's already tight features screwed up in hatred. "It's not your room anymore. I'm kicking you out, effective immediately!"

Paige's blood boiled. "You can't kick me out. It's just as much my room as yours." Her fingers tingled and she was ready to claw the woman's eyes out.

Tia stood firmly in place, holding Paige back. "You don't want to room with this bitch anyway. Get your things and you can move in with me."

"Bitch? Excuse me?" Merline glared down her long nose at Tia.

"Yeah, you heard me. And she's going to sue you for slander unless you can prove she stole money from you or the soldiers' fund." Tia got right up in the woman's face. "If you don't want a whole mess of trouble, you'd better not make any unfounded allegations against my friend or we'll have you for dinner!"

Tia grabbed another box and sashayed down the hall, her head held regally high.

"Well, I nevah!" Merline slammed the door hard enough to break windows all across campus.

Several other students peeked out the cracks of their doors, their wide eyes filled with questions.

"My reputation's shot to hell," Paige murmured under her breath. It would kill her family if they found out and she hoped the news wouldn't travel all the way to Biloxi. But bad news and vicious gossip had a way of beating the fastest jet liner.

"Don't you listen to those gossip-mongers, sweetie. They wouldn't know the truth if it bit them in the butt." Tia tossed the boxes in the trunk of her car and then slid behind the steering wheel.

Despite herself, Paige cracked a grin. She strapped on her seatbelt for the short ride and was surprised when Tia turned the opposite direction from her house and took her to the all-you-could-eat fish camp on the outskirts of town.

"But my diet!" Paige recoiled from the thought of food in general and this high-calorie nightmare in particular.

Tia prodded her toward the sinfully delicious smells of catfish, shrimp, and crab legs basking in rich, creamy butter. The only thing she could possibly eat here without a mountain of guilt was the corn, shrimp and crab, sans butter.

"Seafood's not that bad and besides, you've had a rough day. You can indulge occasionally."

"That's not what you said earlier."

Tia scrunched up her nose. "That's when you only had man troubles to deal with. Now you have real ones."

So was this supposed to be like her last real meal before she was thrown in the slammer? The thought didn't settle well on her stomach. Just in case, she eyed the luscious corn on the cob smothered in butter longingly. She could drown her sorrows in that for a brief respite. And then when she was in jail whiling away the long and lonely hours, she could whittle away at her waist doing sit-ups. She'd come out of that jail with hard abs.

"Dig in," Tia prodded, heaping her plate full of crayfish, catfish and coleslaw, which she topped off with a frothy glass of iced tea.

Paige talked herself into being bad. Eat, drink and be merry, for tomorrow she might lose her freedom.

* * * * *

Danny struggled to put his weight on his bad leg and cursed up a long string of adjectives when it started to buckle. "Hand me the God-blessed crutches," he said to the wary nurse who eyed him dubiously.

He knew he was their worst patient but didn't much care. If they couldn't help him, he wished they'd leave him alone with his misery.

She pushed the wheelchair forward. "I have instructions to take you in this, Captain. If you would…"

He counted to ten under his breath, trying to remember not to kill the messenger. For once he wished he was back in Iraq where at least he'd been ambulatory. Through tight lips, he told her, "I prefer to make it on my own steam," even if that wasn't entirely true. It would be with the aid of the clunky crutches, which he still hadn't mastered.

"Please, Captain. You'll get to walk down in Physical Therapy." A hopeful glint lit the pretty woman's amber eyes but he couldn't give in. It would be like relinquishing his masculinity.

"That's an order, soldier!" an authoritative masculine voice bellowed. "I don't want to catch you giving our nurses a hard time again." His head doctor, a full bird colonel, rifled into the room and stared him down. "Do I make myself clear, Captain?"

Sunlight bounced off his eagles almost blinding Danny who had to squint against the vicious rays. "Perfectly. I mean, yes Sir!" He hobbled over to the chair and plunked his butt firmly on it, another string of expletives strangling in his throat.

"I don't want to hear of this tomfoolery again. If I do, I'll personally place you on report." The colonel pivoted on the ball of his foot, his white lab coat flapping behind him.

"You best listen to him, Cap'n. He means business." The woman wheeled him to his appointment, her rubber-soled nurse's shoes squishing on the newly sterilized linoleum.

What colonel didn't mean what they said? In his experience, the whole passel was anal.

With the whoosh of the elevator doors and a couple of bells later, he was whisked into PT.

A bright-faced, big-toothed major greeted him with sickening-sweet joviality. "And how is the Captain doing today?" he asked as he took responsibility for Danny.

The nurse screwed up her overly bright ruby red lips. "He's surly as ever, I'm afraid. But he's your problem for the afternoon. Call me when he's ready to come back."

"Will do," the therapist said, ignoring Danny's growls. "I'm sure we'll get along right fine."

* * * * *

"Therapy time," the annoyingly cheerful nurse said in a singsong voice as she pushed a wheelchair into the room.

"How're you doing today?"

"Fair to middling," Danny said glaring at the man, negating his words as he chucked his sheet off his legs.

"Let me help you out of bed."

"I can do it myself," he said, growling, trying to scoot to the edge of the bed. When acute pain sliced through him, he grimaced and pulled back

"Stop growling or do I have to give you a distemper shot?" His therapist whistled as he massaged Danny's aching muscles, getting on Danny's nerves. Perpetually happy, too-smiley people usually turned out to be psychopaths and he didn't need one within a mile of his injured leg. He didn't trust unnaturally broad or bright smiles. They might hide a serial killer or megalomaniac. That was one reason he'd always hated clowns and this guy was clownish all right, major or not.

"If I were in your position, I'd have reason to stop growling." Danny grimaced. He hadn't meant to sound whiny. "I meant, if I could stand and move around on my leg like you do. On your legs, I mean." Was his tongue crippled now, too? Seemed that way.

"Stop fighting us and cooperate and you will be." The man motioned for him to roll over on his back.

That was easy for the jerk to say. He didn't feel the pain or lack the strength to perform simple movements. He didn't feel weaker than a newborn.

Putting his weight on his arms, he hoisted himself around. The exertion made him pant. *Great!* Now he couldn't turn over on his own steam either without huffing and puffing. Some military fighting machine he was.

"See? That wasn't so tough. You did that like a pro."

Danny bit back a snarl. Now the man was treating him like a kid.

"Okay, pal. Time for your real workout. Game to try the parallel bars today?

As in spinning around them? It was barely worthwhile walking if he had to hang onto handrails and have a spotter in case he fell. It was only slightly better than crutches. At least the bars didn't kill his armpits. But he could only walk a few feet and couldn't reach any place of interest.

"That's the way! You're doing it!" The major clapped, a regular cheering section.

When the therapist tried to help him off the bars, he spat, "Back off, bubba. I gotta learn to do this on my own. I don't plan to stay in this neck of the woods much longer."

The man held up his hands and took a couple of steps back. "I'm here if you need me, slugger. Don't overdo it and strain yourself. You're making progress."

Danny snorted. Like a tortoise.

"With an injury like yours, recovery doesn't happen overnight. You need patience."

Patience? Meanwhile his family was probably wondering if he'd crawled into a spider hole and Paige had probably written him off for dead. He couldn't blame them but he still wasn't ready to subject them to his surliness or let them know the possibility that he might never walk right again.

Paige. God he missed her. Her letters and support had kept him going in Iraq. But offering her half a man wasn't the way he worked. He wondered what she was doing. Probably fending off handsome, athletic coeds and fraternity men. Dating a different man every night. Or worse, she'd found someone special who would make her forget all about him and Key West.

She had probably erased him from her mind, which, he reminded himself for the millionth time, would be a good thing, not a bad one. If she didn't think about him, she would get over the pain that had etched her face and sliced through him their last night together. She wouldn't worry about him and wonder what he was doing.

Now, if he could forget about Paige… About her lips and her kisses. About all those sexy freckles he hadn't yet memorized. About how sweet and caring she was. About his longing to take her back into his arms and love her all night. Thirsting to forget, he pushed himself. Either he'd learn to walk again and get on with his life or he'd wear himself out so that he'd forget that life was passing him by.

Chapter Nine

Two uniformed policeman awaited Paige outside her auditing class, scaring her half to death. "Please accompany us, Miss Forbes."

Her classmates stared open-mouthed. Neresa from Alpha Psi marched up to her, tossed her platinum blonde hair behind her shoulders and harrumphed. "Is it true you're nothing more than a common thief? If any of the Alpha Psis soldiers' fund is missing, we're pressing charges. Our auditor's going over the books now."

Paige shrunk inside. This blatant scene lent credence to all the rumors. By next class, she would be infamous. Why didn't they just tar and feather her and get it over with?

"Move on, lady." The taller of the two policemen shooed Neresa away, disdain streaking his voice. "No interfering in police business."

Paige chewed her lower lip as she followed the long blue uniform in front of her. This must mean they thought they had found hard evidence. She needed her attorney.

There was no help for it. She had to involve her family attorney.

She became better acquainted with the back of a police car than she'd ever wanted to be and made an insightful discovery about herself—she was claustrophobic. The cage closed in on her and the air smelled thin and stale, reeking of alcohol and tobacco. If they wrecked on the way to the station, there were no handles so she could open the door.

A miniscule town, even compared to Biloxi-Gulfport, the cruiser pulled up at the station after only a couple of traffic lights, of which only one had turned red.

The stockier barrel-chested officer with Dumbo ears opened her door. "Out with you, sweetheart. Don't cause no ruckus and we won't have cause to cuff you."

College student didn't mean dumb and naïve no matter how many locals might think otherwise. She followed mutely, determined not to say one word without solid advice from her family's attorney, her Uncle Jedediah.

The duo flirted with the attractive Hispanic receptionist until the woman blushed prettily. Then they led Paige to a small, dark and smoky room and read her rights. "Are you willing to speak to us without an attorney present?" The big ol' one, who wasn't much wider than a string of spaghetti, leaned over the table and stared her down.

She swallowed hard and shook her head. "Don't I get a phone call? I want my attorney present."

The shorter officer sighed heavily and rose to his full height. He jerked his thumb at the door. "Tell Maria to let her make her call." He sounded as pissed as if he'd just told his partner to take his wife to bed.

She followed the thick-set policeman down the hall, trying not to make eye contact with any of the unsavory characters sprawled across rickety wooden chairs in the hall. Some were handcuffed to their seats and looked as if they'd camped out there all night. Others whistled at her and called obscenities that burned her ears.

"Y'all cut that out," her escort snapped, waving his police stick.

When they reached the phone, he jerked his thumb at it. "You got one call. Ten minutes." He hauled a metal chair from across the room, straddled it backward and watched her closely.

Disconcerted, she dialed her parents, as she didn't know her uncle's number. She swore if she ever got out of here, she'd commit his number to memory. She'd have much preferred speaking to Jed.

Her mother answered, which she should have expected, as it was a workday for her father. Quickly, she outlined her plight, begged their forgiveness for not being upfront about the accusations from the start and requested help.

A graceful woman, her mother promised to bring her father and uncle up to Hattiesburg just as soon as she could round them up. "We love you, precious. Walk with the angels." Her mother didn't believe in saying goodbye. It was too final.

Did angels dare tread here? "I'm done," she said after she wished her mama farewell. Soon as she hung up, she scowled. She should have asked her mama to call Tia and catch her up so as not to worry her when she didn't come home. Not that being locked up in a holding cell wasn't worrisome, but at least she wouldn't call out the state troopers to check ditches for her.

Even if her mama got the men straight away, it was a far piece up the road from Gulfport—a good two hours or better.

"Someone fixin' to come for you?" The squat cop chewed a wad of gum as he spoke, muffling his words.

"My folks and our family counsel." She felt a mite better knowing they were on their way, even if it would be a several-hour wait.

The man scrunched his nose. "Put little missy here in a holding cell." To her he said, "We'll let you know when they arrive."

She was escorted to the back of the jail and put in a cell with two other women, one with a glass eye that gave her the heebie jeebies, and one throw-back flower child who flitted through the cell like a snowflake on acid.

She curled up in the corner on a thin, lumpy mattress, afraid to take her eyes off her cellmates. The cosmic peace lover was probably safe enough although, if she was on an acid trip, who knew? She could be seeing giant white rabbits and all kinds of scary stuff. The Stephen King reject looked as if her teeth might very well be lethal weapons so that she covered her throat best as she could.

Sharp clanking awakened Paige rudely and she jolted up with a start, banging her head on the bunk above her. Disoriented until the fog cleared from her brain, she blinked several times.

"Yo, red. You got visitors in the lobby. Get your freakin' butt over here. I ain't got all day to waste."

When Paige rose and ambled to the exit, the flower child flitted after her, trying to glide out the door.

"This here love-in ain't for you, Daphne." The policeman blocked her way and locked them back in as the old shabby woman cast a hex on him.

"It's Daisy, pig." The flower child pouted, and glowered at him as she played with her love beads.

"Whatevah!" The cop increased his stride so that she almost had to run to catch up. At five-feet-seven-inches, she wasn't a tiny girl nor were her legs short, yet she felt diminutive beside her jailor.

"Oh, honey!" Her mama blinked back tears and rushed to hug her. The embrace was so tight and prolonged, she feared her lungs would collapse.

Paige greeted her parents and finally her uncle, on whom she had pinned all her hopes.

"What's this nonsense about, daughter?" Her father towered over her, his shoulders slightly stooped. There was more gray in his hair than she recalled, unless it was her overactive imagination exaggerating everything.

"It's not nonsense," Jedediah said, opening a file. "They seem to think they have proof that Paige doctored the books and embezzled store funds."

Outrage consumed her all over again and she was about to boil over. "I never! And I told them so in no uncertain terms."

"You should've told us straight away, sugar bug, instead of letting this escalate," her mama said, pain flashing in eyes the shade of maple syrup. "We might've been able to prevent you being put in this…*place*."

"She's right." Her father shoveled his fingers through his still thick and springy hair. "Don't you know you can tell us anything? You've always confided in us before."

Not in a long time and certainly not everything else. Not about Danny. She averted her guilty gaze.

Her mama gave her the once-over and shook her head as she eased her white gloves off her fingers. "Just look at you, worrying yourself to death. Heavens, you'd disappear if you turned sideways. Did you stop eating?"

"I've been dieting and exercising. I wanted to surprise you when I came home at Christmas." All her former pride and joy at losing the weight had disappeared under the upset of her current plight. What good was her struggle if she ended up behind bars?

"You certainly managed to do that." Her father circled her so that she wanted to tighten her wagons.

"Let's get back to the issue at hand," Jed said, flipping open his legal pad. "Who else had access to those funds? Name names."

She rattled off the other employees, ending with Penny, bitterness settling in her heart.

"Any of them acting strangely or different? Any of them suddenly have more money or flashing more trinkets?"

"Penny." The hated name tripped off her tongue without hesitation.

"Uhm…interesting." Jed doodled on his paper.

"What's so damned interesting?" her papa asked, practically snarling. He paced the small room cracking his knuckles, ignoring her mama's reprimanding stare.

Jedediah held up the paper to show two huge 'PFs'. "Paige Forbes and Penny Foster. Both PF."

Intense dislike for Penny roiled in Paige's gut. "She's been flashing a lot of fancy new clothes. We thought maybe she'd found herself a sugar daddy."

Jed narrowed his eyes. "So she doesn't normally have these expensive kinds of things? Do you recall when you first noticed her new wardrobe?"

Paige had pondered it so many times she almost choked on the thought. "It must've been right around the time they say the funds first went missing."

Her uncle scribbled more notes. "I think I'll have to look a lot closer at this young lady. What about the others? Anything suspicious?"

Paige thought back and came up with a blank. Shaking her head, she said, "No. Only about Penny."

"Okay. We've got something to go on. Let's go post her bail and get her out of here."

Bail? "How much is it?"

Her mama shushed her and waved the men on. "Don't you be worrying none about that. Your father will handle it."

Exhaustion made her bones ache and she let it go. It wasn't as if they wouldn't get their money back. She had no plans to flee anywhere except to her nice comfy bed in Tia's cottage.

By ten, when the full moon was high overhead and lit their path, bail was posted and she was given a lift to Tia's house.

Her friend bolted out the door and enveloped her in a fierce hug. "You poor thing. You should sue for unlawful arrest and harassment. Killin' would be too good for the likes of that witch who set you up." Tia blushed and turned to Paige's mother. "I'm sorry, Miss Evelyn. I'm just so riled up."

"We're all upset, dear." Her mama patted Tia's hand comfortingly and bestowed a commiserating smile on her.

Paige's father took out his money clip and handed Tia a wad of bills. "Here, to help out with the bills."

"Thank you, but I can't accept it." Tia stepped back.

Her father pressed it on her. "Then consider it a loan 'til Paige is back at work."

Tia took it reluctantly. "Thank you." Then her father handed her money and half-turned to his brother. "You're a witness where she's getting this money from."

"It'd be better if you wire transfer it to her bank from yours so we can prove where she got it if necessary." Jed kicked a pecan off the sidewalk and stuck his hands in his pockets. "I'm advising this as your attorney. For Tia, too, as she may come under future scrutiny."

Her father scowled, his broad forehead a sea of wrinkles. "What's this world coming to when a man can't even give his own family money?"

Jed pursed his lips and shrugged his thin shoulders.

"We're going to get us a hotel room and we'll see you tomorrow. Sleep tight, sugar bug," her father said, kissing her cheek.

Unrelenting, Tia demanded a full accounting, keeping her up 'til the wee hours of the morning with her inquisition.

* * * * *

"What you doing lounging around in that hospital bed?" Jimmy's voice flowed over the phone.

Danny perked up and scooted up in his bed, causing his sheet to bunch up around his waist. It had been ages since he'd heard Jim's voice and it warmed his soul as not much else had been able to do of late.

"How'd you know I was here?" Danny aimed the remote control at the TV mounted high on the wall and shut it off.

"I have my sources. Why are you there, man?"

"Didn't your *sources* tell you?" He wondered who the source was.

"Something about your leg but nothing specific. What happened to it?"

"Enemy bullet got me." He left out the part about chasing Jimmy's sister and falling down the stairs like a complete cretin.

"Tough luck, dude. But the leg will be okay, won't it? I mean, they didn't…"

"Amputate it?" Danny rubbed his throbbing appendage. Meds would take the edge off the pain but he didn't want to become addicted to them. "No. Nothing so radical. But it doesn't want to work right, neither. Don't tell your sister, okay?"

There was a long pause. "My sister. You mean…you…and…she? When did this happen?"

"You didn't know?" He bit his tongue. Of course, Jim didn't know. Until Key West it had been just a mail thing.

"No one tells me anything. Just like Paige waited 'til now to tell us about the passel of trouble she's in…"

Danny's heart skipped several beats and then sped up. "What kind of trouble?"

"I take that back. Nobody tells anybody anything."

"Tell me!" Danny roared into the phone, awakening his roommate, a Gulf War veteran who just had a knee replacement. "Sorry, bubba," he said to the fellow who grunted and turned his face away from the light.

"Maybe I shouldn't…"

"I swear you tell me now or I'll…"

"Feel better, dude. Gotta run." The phone line went dead.

Danny muttered a string of curses and then dialed Tia's house. "What's going on with Paige?"

"I can't tell you." Tia sounded a lot more distant than mere miles could account for. She practically froze him out.

"Jimmy says she's in some sort of trouble."

Silence hung heavy on the line. Finally the woman spoke over the crackling static. "She doesn't want you to know anymore than you don't want her to know. She's sworn me to secrecy."

"Does Leo know?" *Christ!* Everybody knew Paige's secret but him. Bitterness and agitation warred inside him, twisting his gut.

"She doesn't want him knowing either. I'd better go before she overhears us."

"She's not hurt, is she?" His lungs grew tight as very real fear gripped him.

"Depends on what you mean by that. Not physically." Pots and pans clanged in the background and then whooshing water almost drowned out Tia's hushed tones. "She's coming. Bye."

He breathed easier although he wondered at Tia's meaning. "Have her call me at 555-555-5555." He swore when the line went dead before he had finished the phone number.

What kind of trouble could Paige possibly be in? Maybe his parents knew. His mother and Miss Evelyn were tight. He called home and got the scoop from his sister, aka the voice of Biloxi.

Paige jailed? Accused of embezzlement? Facing possible long-term imprisonment? This couldn't be his Paige and yet it was.

He gritted his teeth with determination and hoisted himself out of bed. Sharp pain shot through his leg but he forced himself forward bracing against the wall for support.

The whisper of rubber soles warned him of enemy presence a moment before the nurse's clear voice rang out. "What do you think you're doing, Captain?" The tiny nurse blocked his way, anchoring her hands on her hips.

He refused to flinch and masked his expression so she couldn't see his pain. "I'm leaving. A friend's in trouble."

"You'll be AWOL, Sir. I can't let you."

He'd forgotten he was still in the Army, he'd been stateside and bed-bound so long, and he bit back a wrathful curse. "I need leave."

"It takes time to process leave requests. And what about your physical therapy?" She asked with a trace of sarcasm.

He smiled smugly at the uppity nurse. "I can do therapy as an outpatient and this is an emergency."

She shrugged. "You'll have to clear it with your doctor and your commanding officer."

"Would you let the doctor know I need to see him soon as he comes in?" He gazed out the window at much longed-for freedom, wondering how much-longer it would be 'til he gained his, and if Paige would lose hers.

"Will you get back in that bed?" She didn't budge an inch.

Determination welling in his chest, he lowered himself to the mattress and lifted his leg up, inch by excruciating inch, as his breath hissed in. He had to manage his movement and pain better or he'd be no good to himself or Paige. He'd felt sorry for himself too long. It was time to snap back to reality and get on with his life. He was sick of hospital beds and wasting away. Days droned into nights, which droned into weeks and then months. Before he knew it, it would be years — unless he did something about it right here and now.

The doctor didn't show up 'til the next day when Danny had about decided he had received a silent denial of request. These walls, the emasculating gowns and lights out so early were driving him crazy. His mind was turning to mush being holed up in here.

The colonel pulled his sheet down and examined his leg. "What's this I hear that you want to take leave now?"

"I have an emergency I need to take care of, Sir."

"How well are you walking on the leg?"

Danny thought about lying but figured the doctor had all his particulars in his file. "Not 100% yet but I'm working on it."

"How do you plan to work on it if you leave us?"

Hope flared in his chest. "As an outpatient. My family lives in Biloxi and so I can still come to the physical therapy clinic regularly."

The doctor pursed his lips thoughtfully.

The colonel pulled up a chair beside him and treated him to a piercing glare. "What happened to the young man who didn't want his family to know about his injuries?" The inquisitive man sounded more like a psychiatrist than an orthopedist.

Paige's image flashed in front of Danny's eyes and his heart flipped over in his chest. "My girl's in trouble. She needs me."

"She in the family way?" A small frown of disapproval tugged at the colonel's lips.

Danny tried not to fidget but it was hard to remain still under such direct fire. "No, Sir. It's not like that. She's in some serious legal trouble."

"Sorry to hear that, son. I'm going to approve leave providing you set up an outpatient therapy schedule before we discharge you. People always recover quicker in the bosom of a supportive family. You may have been out of here by now if you'd told them earlier."

Danny breathed a sigh of relief. "Thank you, Sir. About how long will it take?" His battle was only half-won. The Army was known to take a notoriously long time to perform the simplest of tasks unless it benefited them.

"I'll try to have it expedited."

"I'd appreciate that, Sir." He itched to find Paige and get the whole skinny.

The man hitched up his slacks and stood, blocking out the sun streaming through the window. "Just promise me one thing, Captain." The colonel gazed down at him with a fatherly air about him.

"If I can, Sir." The afternoon sun glaring through the window made him squint when the colonel moved to the side.

"Take good care of your lady and get walking again. You and your lady deserve the best."

Technically that was two promises but Danny wasn't going to argue with a superior officer, especially not when he agreed with both. "Will do."

The colonel saluted. "Carry on, Captain."

Overjoyed that he was getting sprung, Danny saluted back with a grin. "Yes, Sir!"

Chapter Ten

Jedediah clasped Paige's hands and squeezed, his gaze flat and dull. "I have to be honest with you. The prosecution's building a strong case against you."

"Isn't it just circumstantial?" Paige's breath caught in her throat and she stared at her uncle incredulously.

"They have your initials. You signed off on the petty cash when it wasn't correct." Jed's take on her plight seemed to seal her miserable fate.

A major headache pounded against her temples. *She'd been a fool.* She should've told Paul immediately when the books didn't balance. She suspected a good many fools were in jail. *A cursed day it was when she'd decided to become an accountant!* "So what can we do now?"

"Find the real culprit. Catch her dead to rights."

Penny had framed her but good. "Precisely how do we catch her?" She rested her elbows on the table and leaned forward, anxious to hear.

Jed patted her hand. "Just let me worry about that. I'm looking into Miss Foster's affairs. If I told you exactly what, you might slip and alert her and she'll cover her tracks."

Paige scowled. "I have no plans to go near that bi-witch. She's not exactly one of my favorite people."

"Promise me you'll take my advice and let me handle it. Don't do or say anything to alert her."

Paige massaged her throbbing head. "I promise." How did he expect her not to worry when he said himself the prosecution had a good case? She hugged her uncle and bid him adieu, then made her way toward home.

Her cell phone shrilled and she flipped it open. Tia's number read out on the display. She put it up to her ear and asked, "Where are you?"

"On my way home. I just left my uncle." One good thing about Hattiesburg, you could walk almost anywhere within half an hour.

"Hurry up, I have a surprise for you."

Tia's voice was too buttery, too sugary. Something was up. What kind of surprise? Did she want to know? None of them had been good of late, even if they appeared so at first sight. She had learned not to trust the combination of Tia and surprises. She was in enough trouble.

"On second thought, I think I'll stay out a while longer." *A lot longer.*

"No! You have to come home." Desperation threaded Tia's voice and she murmured something unintelligible. Another muffled voice answered her.

"Who's there? The police?" Her forehead puckering, she pondered who would constitute a surprise. Not her parents as they were already in town. So was her uncle.

Who else would visit? *Leo?* He wouldn't be a surprise for her. *Danny?* Why now after all this time? She crossed them off her list.

Who else? That left only Jimmy. He made the most sense out of anyone on her list. She changed her mind. She really needed her big brother at a time like this.

Excitement thrummed through her veins. She'd not seen Jimmy in months and he had been absent of late on email, too. "It's Jimmy, isn't it? Don't lie or I'm turning around and not coming home."

"Brat." Tia sighed deeply. "Okay, you ruined your own surprise."

"Put him on the phone." Trusting Tia still didn't come easily and she mourned her former trust in her best friend. Trust was so easy to lose and took so long to rebuild.

More murmured voices came across the line, and then Jim's. "That's a fine welcome, refusing to come home and see me. You sure know how to pull the welcome mat out from under a guy's feet."

So much for gracious Southern hospitality. "I thought you might be someone else." She didn't want to face Danny, as highly unlikely it was that he would want to see her.

He paused so long she was afraid he'd hung up. She quickened her pace and turned onto Hardy Street. "Jimmy?"

"I'm here. I was just checking to see if I'm still me."

Vintage Jimmy. She swallowed a laugh so as not to encourage any more of his shenanigans. "Good," she murmured dryly. "It took long enough to get used to the way you are."

She could see the house and frowned at the absence of Jimmy's car in the drive. The smart aleck must've parked on another street and walked over to catch her unawares.

A few seconds later, she let herself in the house and tackled Jimmy in a big hug, afraid to let go in case he was an illusion. Anything was possible the way her life had been going of late.

"Whoa! I'm happy to see you, too, but don't strangle me." Contrary to his words, he whirled her around until she was dizzy.

When he set her down on her feet, the room was still spinning and she stumbled against her brother who righted her and kept a steadying hand on her. Blinking, she tried to clear her fuzzy vision.

After the haze burned away, she was face-to-face with Danny and she gaped. Then she turned an accusing stare on her so-dead roommate. "You lied."

Tia came over to her and placed her hands on Paige's shoulders and looked her squarely in the eyes. "No, I didn't. Jimmy is here. You and Danny need to talk so I'm going to show Jimmy around town."

Paige swallowed hard. "You can't leave!" On a hiss, she accused, "You told him."

Jimmy stepped forward matter-of-factly. "I told him. Tia's right. It's past time the two of you had a heart-to-heart."

Tia hugged her and whispered in her ear, "At least hear him out, sweetie. He's gone through a lot, too."

What did that cryptic remark mean? She eyed Danny with her peripheral vision, trying to assess what was different about him that she couldn't pinpoint. Probably nerves, like her. But no, Tia was alluding to more than apprehension.

She nodded at Tia, deciding to act adult even if her stomach felt queasy and her head was still spinning. It wouldn't do to let Danny see her in an unfavorable light even though they were through. She had to salvage some dignity.

Paige nodded to Tia and Jimmy. "All y'all don't stay out all night." She perched on the recliner so Danny wouldn't try to sit beside her. She didn't think she could stand it if he brushed against her or tried to take liberties. Her heart was way too raw and the wounds he'd inflicted, still weeping. To hide the fact that moths were flittering about in her stomach, she folded her hands on her knees and pressed her thumbs together, a trick she'd been taught when very young.

Danny limped to the couch across from her and lowered himself. *Limped?* The injury to his leg was much worse than he had let on.

Her heart ascended into her throat. "You weren't completely straight with me about your leg, were you? You were hurt pretty badly."

All blood drained from Danny's face and she was afraid he'd pass out. He was whiter than the magnolias blooming outside the front window.

"It was on the mend when I went to Key West. Then it got, uh, re-injured and I've been out of commission for some time."

"You didn't want me to know?" Her thoughts jumped ahead linearly at light speed. "And you didn't want to see me." She should have been the first one he called for when he needed someone. He had never cared for her. Not in the same way she'd cared for him. Though she had suspected as much, the naked truth still sliced and she bled profusely inside.

Had he called for Penny?

She mashed her thumbs together so hard they ached, as she awaited his reply. Then why was he here? What was possibly left to say? *I enjoyed screwing you and your hot friend. Let's have another gangbang.* She'd murder Jimmy for bringing the man by here if that's what he wanted. Rage began to boil deep in her core as she recalled that disastrous, devastating night.

"I didn't want *you* to see me this way. You deserve better than half a man. I could be crippled the rest of my life." He fingered a shiny cane that leaned beside him on the couch.

Shocked, she bit back a gasp. Danny, crippled? How much pain was he in?

Pity and fury warred within her. Licking her lips, she sought appropriate words. "Why ever would you think that I would love you any less, or think you any less of a man?" *Bless the daft man's heart. Had he sustained a brain injury, too?*

Danny studied the handle of his cane as if he could divine the mysteries of the universe in its depths. Then he lifted his clear gray gaze and pierced her clear to her core. "Your pity's the last thing I want. You deserve a complete man that can love and satisfy you the way you deserve, one with better judgment than I showed down in the Keys."

She winced at mention of the Keys. Much as it had pained her afterward, she had been a willing, even eager, participant, too. Her sense of honor wouldn't allow him to take full blame. Squaring her shoulders, she met his gaze straight on. "We all got carried away. I consented too." To be completely truthful, she had indulged first.

A slow burn crept into her cheeks at remembrance of being fucked by two virile men at once and her panties started getting wet. *What a wanton slut she was. Her pussy craved more wild sex even as her heart broke.*

Down girl! She ordered, veiling her eyes with a sweep of her lashes lest he read what was in her mind.

His knuckles whitened on his cane and he shifted his bulk back on the couch. "That wasn't my only lapse in judgment."

Her brow quirked at that. *What else wasn't she privy to?* Had he, Tia and Leo *partied* all night after her exit? If so, she didn't want to know. She refused to prod him for more details.

After several moments, he cleared his throat and coughed. "I ran after you..."

He had? She peered at him closely as her heart leapt with joy and her pulse raced.

"But I fell down the stairs. My damned leg went out."

She gasped and didn't bother quelling it this time. "Oh my God!"

His eyes glassy, he stared into space as if looking into an agonizing past. "Leo and Tia found me and had me taken to the hospital. I'd really wrecked my leg and it had to be operated on the next morning. I've been laid up in that hospital ever since."

She was going to kick Tia's bony butt into next week for not telling her. Maybe into next year. Right after she smacked herself for thinking the worst of Danny. *She was such a fool.*

She moved over to the couch by his side and hugged him. "I'm so sorry..."

He pulled back with a growl. "I don't want your pity."

She smiled at the dear, silly man, as her eyes adored his beloved face, which was still heart-stoppingly devastating despite a five-o'-clock shadow and lean cheeks. *Well, perhaps because of the sexy stubble.* She wondered how it would feel against her soft flesh…between her legs…

A heat wave rippled through her hotter than the most sweltering Delta day. It was all she could do to quell the rampaging desire and not ravage him right here on the couch. "Pity's the last thing I'm feeling," she said with a wicked wink. A little anger remained, but was rapidly being drowned by red-hot desire. Pity didn't begin to enter the mix.

But she had to know why he was here now. Obviously not to ravage her. There was no matching passion in his eyes. "So why the change of heart? Why are you telling me now?"

Anger glittered in his eyes as he turned slowly and painfully toward her. "I heard you were in trouble…"

"So you pity me," she drawled and scooted away from him. *Priceless.* He could feel sorry for her but she wasn't allowed the same consideration.

He followed her, trapping her against the end of the couch. "It's not pity. Can't a man want to protect his woman?"

His woman? Tingles raced down her spine and she wondered if she had rightly heard him. She didn't want to be jumping to conclusions. Then the rest of his words registered. "And vice versa? Can't a woman want to support her man?"

Danny stared at her for a long time while she held her breath. "What good would a one-sided relationship be? We have to take turns being strong for the other." What man wanted a shallow, self-centered partner? *No man she could truly love or respect.*

She tried another argument. "Do you want a clinging vine, or a strong woman who loves you?" Since long before the Scarlett O'Haras, southern women had been a hearty lot and she was proud of her heritage.

"Would you want a bitter, whimpering man?" Unmistakable bitterness laced his voice.

"No," she shot back, lifting her jaw high.

"Then you wouldn't have wanted me how I was all those months I was laid up. I had enough pity to make up for everyone. My only redeeming virtue, I thought, is that I wouldn't be bastard enough to subject you to it. Not now, and certainly not forever. I didn't want you to end up a miserable wretch like me. I didn't want you to wake up one day and hate my guts and loathe your life with me."

"That could never happen." Immense love swelled in her heart as she cupped his rough cheek in her palm, adoring the feel of it. At great risk to her heart, she admitted, "You're my sunshine. You're the stars and moon in my heaven. You always have been." She moved her hand to his heart. "It's what's in here..." she touched his injured leg tenderly, "Not here, that I love."

A mischievous twinkle lit Danny's eyes and he looked down at the swelling in his pants. With a sly grin, he said, *soto voce*, "So you don't care about what's down there?"

Her gaze followed his and juices flowed hot from her tingling pussy. "Don't go twisting my words. I like that *very* much."

He pressed her back against the arm of the couch. "Only *like*?"

She quickly amended her error as she gazed deeply into his darkening passion-glazed eyes. "I love it. Better?"

"I think you'd better show me." His hot breath fanned her neck and then he licked it sensually. She trembled as wild fire blazed through her veins.

Writhing, she tried to wriggle out from under him. "We'd better take this into my room so we don't give my brother an eyeful when he gets back."

"I wish I could carry you, darlin'…" Disappointment trailed off in his voice.

She didn't need a caveman or a swashbuckler, just Danny. Linking her fingers through his, she led him to her boudoir and locked the door. This time, she wanted him all to herself. She was much too greedy to share.

"Come here." Danny pulled her into his arms and teased her lips tenderly. "You're the stars and moon and sun in my heaven, too." He sifted his fingers through her heavy fall of hair. "You can't imagine how many nights I wished I was here, holding you like this, or paying up on all those kisses I owe you…or connecting the dots."

Against his lips, she murmured, "I imagine it was about as many nights as I yearned for you. I can hardly believe you're here."

He nibbled her ear and then licked his way down the arch of her neck. "I still can't fathom my shy girl traipsed naked around Key West."

She pouted prettily and said huskily, "I was in costume. Didn't you like it?"

A primitive growl rumbled deep in his chest and he dipped his tongue into the vee of her blouse, making her writhe. "I loved it—but I want to see the real you—all of you."

Thrilled, yet apprehensive, she hesitated. She wasn't possessed of clear, alabaster flesh like most Mississippi magnolias. She was more like a Mississippi mud pie she had so many freckles. Perhaps they should wait for it to turn dark and keep the lights out.

"I think I hear Tia and Jim returning." She tried to pull back and was instantly struck by how chilly it was outside the circle of his arms.

He pulled her back and heated up his seduction, unbuttoning her shirt slowly, feathering hot kisses down her chest. "I plan on kissing each and every freckle before we leave this room." He backed her to the bed. "But not while standing up… Can't have my leg giving out on us at a crucial moment."

A purr tickled her throat as she stretched out on her bed and held her arms out to him. "That would never do, soldier."

"Not at all." After divesting her of her clothes and attempting to connect the dots, he rolled onto his back, dragging in air. "I'm afraid the old leg doesn't want to cooperate." Anguish contorted his features and he swore under his breath.

If she didn't do something drastic to help him now, he might never open up to her again. "It just needs practice. *Lots* of practice." She hoped they'd be given the opportunity, that she wouldn't be behind bars, unable to feel the sanctity and passion of being held in his arms.

"How's this?" she asked, about as innocent as pure sin. Straddling him gingerly, she rubbed her pussy across the velvety tip of his penis. Pure longing slammed into her and it took everything she had to grapple with her passion and remain gentle when all she wanted to do was to ride him like the wind.

He moaned his pleasure. "So far, so good." He thrust off the bed, just inserting the tip of his cock into her pussy, parting her labia while his thumb massaged her clit.

Her blood humming fast and feverishly, she cleaved to him. Holding her weight on her arms so as not to hurt his leg, she rode his fully aroused cock.

"Afraid you'll damage the goods?" A light sweat gleaned on his brow and he ground his hips against hers, shooting thrills through her. "I'm not that frail."

Powerful and masterful, he had erased all thought of his injury from her mind. Desperate hunger consumed her and she increased her rhythm, milking his cock.

Bending low to drink of his lips, she molded her breasts to him. Delicious shivers ran through her when his thick mat of hair tickled her nipples.

"Uhm. You taste so good," he murmured against her lips, a breathless catch in his voice. His movements became frantic and he thrust into her powerfully, shuddering.

On the brink of climax, she ground against him until the floodgates opened and rapture rippled through her. She partook of his lips again, their tongues mating.

Breathing hard, he released her lips and nuzzled her nose with his. Stroking her hair softly, he murmured huskily, "You're exquisite."

Dismounting, she snuggled up to his side, stretching her arm over his chest. She found immense delight in the fact that she fit perfectly into the nook of his arm. "Where do you go from here? What's your prognosis?" Her gaze studied the angry crimson scar marring his thigh. He could have been killed and she thanked God that he had escaped a far worse fate.

Her heart went out to him, knowing he wasn't so grateful. She couldn't blame him for she wasn't grateful about the trouble she found herself in, either.

"The docs say I have a long road of physical therapy ahead. They can't promise me that I'll be able to walk normally again although if I work hard, I could possibly walk without a cane someday." He gazed deeply into her eyes. "Can you love a man who can't walk well, much less run or do a number of physically challenging tasks?"

Paige spread her hands over his strongly beating heart. "I love *you*. No matter what."

She chewed her lower lip as her dark future weighed on her heavily. "Can you love a convicted criminal? A prisoner? I could be locked away for a long time."

Danny pulled her tighter against his heart and rocked her gently. "You're not guilty and we're going to fight for your freedom every step of the way."

His assurances lightened her heart only slightly. Now that she knew the wonder of his kisses, of being in his arms, letters wouldn't suffice. She'd lose her mind if she couldn't be with him every day, sleep in his arms every night.

"How much did Jimmy and Tia tell you?"

"Tia didn't tell me anything. She kept your confidence. And Jimmy only told me that your attorney thinks you're being framed. He didn't say how."

She opened her mouth to tell him about Penny's duplicity, but had second thoughts about it. He wouldn't thank her for it.

The door slammed. "Anyone here? Paige? Dan?" Jimmy's easy lope grew louder as he approached their door. "Y'all in there?"

Danny kissed the tip of her nose. "Guess that's our summons."

She pursed her lips never wanting to leave Danny's arms. "Maybe he'll go away if we don't make a peep."

"If you don't put on your clothes, I won't be able to keep my hands off and you're not very quiet." Mirth danced across his eyes and curled his lips upward.

With mock outrage she sat up and hit him square in the chest with her pillow. "Do my ears deceive me or was I just insulted?"

He caught her to him and crushed her against his chest. Drinking deeply of her lips, he silenced her quite effectively. When he released them, he murmured huskily, "Anything but an insult. But there'd be no doubt what we were doing."

Which reminded her of Tia and how she hadn't had any such inhibitions, had in fact set up their *ménage à trois* or whatever a foursome would be called.

Danny slid his finger under her chin and lifted her face so that he could gaze into her eyes. "Why the haunted look?"

"Did you want Tia, too? Is my love enough to satisfy you?" She held her breath for his answer.

Anguish mixed with firm resolve etched his features. "That night was a huge mistake. You're everything I want. All I desire. And I hope and pray I'm all that you want, too." He pressed her back into the mattress and his swelling cock nestled between her legs.

"I thought you wanted to get dressed and go out there?" Breathing a sigh of relief, she writhed beneath him, spreading her legs wide and rubbing against him, trembling.

"Let 'em wait." He thrust into her so deeply she gasped and held him tightly, matching his powerful rhythm.

Loud moans erupted from her innermost core before she could smother them but, ever helpful, Danny captured the next set with his all-consuming kiss.

Half an hour later when they finally emerged, showered and dressed, their hair still damp, Jimmy and Tia exchanged knowing looks. "I see you're *talking* again."

"Bite me," she mouthed to Tia, grinning ear to ear.

Danny pulled Paige close against his side. "Isn't that what you had in mind?"

Tia set a tray of hors d'oeuvres on the coffee table and then leaned against the arm of her favorite lounger as she nibbled on a mini-quiche. "We need to powwow."

Paige shot her a quelling look, her brows knitting together. Jedediah had warned her to let him handle everything and not to discuss it with anyone. Normally she would share everything with him but she wasn't sure if he still had feelings for Penny. He might think her jealousy of his former girlfriend was at the base of her suspicions.

That grabbed the men's undivided attention and their gazes riveted on her. "You have any theories about who's framing Paige? Or why?"

Paige interrupted them. "Jed advised me against discussing this. He's handling it."

Danny looked up at her, as his thumb caressed the top of her hand. "I want to be with you the next time you meet with him."

Paige began to feel green. Considering Danny had history with Penny she didn't think it advisable. Jed wouldn't feel it wise. "I don't think that's a good idea."

Danny pulled back fractionally. "Why not? Am I not part of the family?"

Her heart pounded rapidly. *Family?* Like part of a big family that included best friends and neighbors? Or family, as in fiancé?

When she hesitated, he supplied, "I've known you since you were knee-high to a bullfrog. We grew up next door to each other."

Was that all? After all they'd been through, he saw her as a little sister? Well, he certainly didn't seem like her big brother. There was no more time to waste. He was pushing the boundaries so she had a right to know. As carefully as she could, she said, "If you were my fiancé, I'm sure he'd have no objection to you being included."

Danny stared and his jaw worked but no sound came out. He had that deer-in-the-headlights look that didn't bode well for her heart and she held her breath. Finally, he asked, "Fiancé? Uh, I'm not sure we're ready for that. I've only recently come home. We have a lot of issues to work out…"

Her heart plummeted to her feet. She had been ready for months. What issues, besides the obvious one that she might go to jail? "Like?"

Danny scowled and shoveled his fingers through his hair. "Your legal troubles. I'm just home from the war and having to start all over…"

Groveling for help wasn't her way but she sucked up her pride and bared her heart. "I could really use some support."

Danny looked away, refusing to meet her gaze. "I'm not able to give you the kind of support you need or deserve."

She gave him one final chance, steeling her heart and soul. Their future was too important to muck up over silly misunderstandings or unspoken sentiments. "You mean financially?"

"Financially or emotionally."

So that was that. A personally delivered "Dear Jane" letter. Enemy fire would have been kinder than this betrayal. Folding her arms over her chest, ordering the stinging tears to stay in her eyes where they wouldn't humiliate her, she stared at him. "Well, don't let me keep you." He obviously didn't want any clinging vines.

"Perhaps we need some time to get our heads together." Yet Danny didn't move for several seconds.

Finally, Paige pointed at the front door. "The door is that way, soldier."

Danny looked from her to the door and back. "Paige…" He paused as if he was going to say more, but then a shutter slammed down over his features. "I'll give you a call later."

Paige just nodded briskly. After he was out of hearing distance, she mumbled, "Don't let it hit you on the way out."

Jimmy frowned as he bent to kiss her cheek. "You sure about this, sis?"

She glared at Danny's retreating back, unable to miss his slow pace as he tried not to limp overly much, trying to still her traitorous heart from reaching out to him. "It's not solely my decision. At least now I'll stop deluding myself about his feelings for me."

Her brother shook his head. "Keep an open mind. He's still not himself."

So she couldn't trust anything he'd said today. She'd remember that. She didn't need any more pain.

"I hope he doesn't say anything to Penny," she mumbled aloud as she waved a sad goodbye to her brother.

"I'd forgotten he knew Penny." Misery and self-deprecation laced Tia's usually chipper tones, sounding alien.

Paige closed the door with a soft, but definite, click. "Remember that I told you that they dated for several years."

"No wonder she hates you. Her little girl isn't his, is she?" Tia fluffed the pillows on the couch, flopped down and rested her feet on the table, her direct gaze dissecting Paige.

No. What a ridiculous notion. No one had ever accused Danny of having a child. Supposedly Penny had ditched him for her child's papa. Now she wondered. "No. He would've told me. He wouldn't abandon his child." Of course he wouldn't. Danny might not be ready to make a commitment to her so soon after his homecoming but he would never abandon his own baby.

"Maybe he refused to acknowledge she was his. Maybe he doesn't know."

Paige didn't want to hear this and shook her head. "Why would you think this?"

Tia played with the tassels on the pillow and shrugged. "You said they dated and the father is out of the picture."

"That's not hard evidence." Just as the evidence against her wasn't hard, either. Still, it niggled at her mind. Was it possible?

No! Danny wasn't like that—even if he was commitment phobic…

An hour later, she faced her uncle, her nerves jumpy. He leaned back in his swivel chair, studying her.

Jumpy, her mind still half with Danny, she tucked her legs under her chair and smoothed the wrinkles from her slacks. "Have you found out anything to help me?"

"Not good." Jed turned to stare out at the waning day. His reflection in the window did not bode well.

"Yes, but I'm awaiting confirmation—*if* she didn't find out what we're doing and cover her tracks." Warning echoed in her uncle's voice.

"What is that?" Curiosity ate at her and she chafed in the soft chair despite how comfy it was.

"I prefer not to say 'til I have proof. We can't afford any mistakes."

Unhappy but understanding, Paige nodded. "Any news about a trial date?"

"Not yet. I'll let you know. Don't say anything else to anybody, you hear?"

"Loud and clear." *She heard all right.* Deflated, she strolled through the campus on the way home. Sight of the Student Union depressed her even more and she turned her back on it. She wished she'd never heard of the computer store or Penny Foster. She wished she'd never set foot on USM soil. She wished she was hell and gone from Mississippi.

Chapter Eleven

The phone roused Paige from her studies a few days later as she prepared for finals. She was of a mind to ignore it but hoped it would be good news about her case. Her uncle's name lit up on the Caller ID so she snatched it up. "Any news?"

"Put on a nice suit and I'll pick you up in forty-five minutes. We have to meet with the campus controller and auditor."

That didn't bode well. "Not the police?"

"No. I'll fill you in on the way." Jed hung up without further embellishment.

She didn't have any decent business suits that remotely fit her since she'd lost the weight. She'd been waiting 'til she reached her goal weight to buy anything so expensive. More recently she had waited so it wouldn't appear she was spending ill-gotten funds. Stressing out, she said aloud to herself, "I have nothing to wear."

Tia startled Paige when she spoke lowly by her ear. "What do you need?"

"A suit or a decent dress. Jed and I have to meet with the campus authorities today."

"You're about a size eight, now. Right? Follow me." Tia led the way to her closet and flung it open to reveal an impressive wardrobe. She extracted a light gray three-piece suit. "Try this on. It'll compliment your coloring."

It was a bit tight but the buttons closed without gaping so it would do. She'd feel quite chic if acid wasn't eating at her stomach. Without proper shoes, purse and hairstyle, she'd look quite gauche.

Tia was a step ahead of her and pulled out matching accessories. "Let me pull your hair into a French twist. It'll be trés chic."

Paige didn't recognize the woman who stared back at her in the mirror a half hour later. Foundation masked her riotous freckles. Dainty pearl earrings leant a touch of elegance to the starchy business suit. Italian leather pumps set off the outfit to perfection. She was primed for her execution, outwardly anyway. Inside, she was a jumble of nerves.

"You look stunning." Tia clapped her hands and circled her, approval lighting her eyes. "You're a woman to reckon with. I wish I could be there for you. Know I'll be there in spirit."

"I know." Paige hugged her friend and then heard the crunch of gravel on the pavement heralding her uncle's arrival. Punctual as always, she saw, vastly relieved that he would be at her side.

"I'll be waiting here for news. Don't leave me hanging." Tia followed her to the door, her fingers curling around the frame.

"I'll let you know the outcome as soon as I'm able." She inhaled deeply, held her head high, and joined her uncle under the cloudy sky.

"You're looking good, Paige. I think you'll be pleased."

"I will?" Her heart thudded against and her ribs. "How pleased?"

"We'll be there in just a couple minutes. You'll learn everything." Rain drizzled on the windshield and he turned on the windshield wipers, mesmerizing her.

Dreading this meeting, she wrung her hands together. Even the sky wept for her. Not a good omen. "You can't tell me anything?"

Jed pulled into a parking space across from the Business Office and cut the ignition. "We're due upstairs in five minutes. Come along." Grimacing, he popped a black umbrella open and held it over her door as she alighted from the car. They tried to dodge the raindrops but they still pelted them. Once inside, he closed the umbrella and escorted her to the Business Office. He schooled his features and then rapped his knuckles sharply on the smoky glass door.

When it opened, she was confronted not only with the controller, auditor and business office manager but her ex-boss, and Penny. All eyes turned on them, Penny's glittering with hatred. Feeling claustrophobic, Paige hesitated on the threshold. The assemblage didn't look as if they had good news to impart.

"Please come inside and close the door," Lucy said.

Jed motioned for Paige to sit before the large oak desk and he took the chair between Paige and Penny, who continued to glare at her.

The controller rose, cleared her throat and looked squarely at Paige. "We'd like to offer our apologies to you. We know now you didn't take any university funds. We've found the guilty party."

A whoosh of relief rushed out of Paige's lungs. She wasn't going to jail and her future wasn't wrecked. But she still stood firm that she would never handle other people's money again. She licked her dry lips. "Am I permitted to know what happened?" *They'd better fill her in after all this!*

All gazes shifted to Penny as Paige expected they would. Lucy nodded to Penny. "You have something to say to Paige."

Penny fidgeted in her seat. "I forged your initials and your name. I stole the money. I'm sorry." She didn't sound remorseful that she had tried to hurt Paige, only that she'd been caught.

What was Paige supposed to say and do now? Forgive her? Forget the woman had tried to ruin not only her career but also her life? She turned her gaze to her uncle. "So Penny will be prosecuted for the crimes?"

The controller spoke up, cutting off her uncle. "No. The university is accepting apologies and financial recompense. We're not pressing charges and Penny will be permitted to graduate with her class."

Penny smiled smugly as if it were all a huge joke.

"But you put me in jail for the same thing. My family had to pay bail, hire an attorney. I don't think you'd have let me graduate."

Her former accusers' eyes shifted away guiltily, giving her the vile answer.

Fuming, she jumped to her feet, scraping the chair back noisily on the old linoleum. "And what about the fact she tried to ruin my life? Doesn't that count for anything? That's worse than embezzling funds…"

Lucy sighed and tucked her hair behind her ears. "She's a single mother trying to support a child on less than minimum wage."

Penny fluttered her eyelashes at Paige. "You'd want the mother of Danny's child to go to jail and lose custody, wouldn't you?"

Danny's child?

Paige froze, unable to breathe. So Tia had been right. How had she been so blind? Penny had probably planned this from day one when she'd helped Paige get hired on at the computer store. A sucker punch to the gut couldn't hurt more.

"If she's Danny's daughter, why isn't he acknowledging her?" Every one in the room faded except her archrival.

Penny shrugged. "Why don't you ask him? He's not the knight in shining armor you think he is."

Jed nudged Paige and grasped her elbow. "Time to go, Paige. This isn't the place."

Paige snapped back to the present and reeled on her heel and broke away from Jed's hold. She marched out of the putrid room, her head held high and her heels banging the floor. "Unbelievable!" Fury ate at her. How could the university and, in particular, her uncle, let Penny off the hook so easily?

When they were outside, she reeled on him, oblivious to the rain. "I can't believe you're okay with this. They only suspected me and had me arrested. They know she did it and don't even slap her hand. What kind of justice is that?"

Jed didn't speak 'til they were enclosed in the vehicle. He turned on the heater and then glanced over his shoulder before merging into traffic. "Life's not fair. I'm just happy you're no longer on the hook."

"But that reprehensible woman deliberately tried to frame me! It was premeditated!" Seething, well past her boiling point, it was a wonder the car's metal didn't melt.

"She has a child depending on her. They see a desperate mother trying to support her daughter."

She bit back a snort. "They didn't see all her posh purses and glitzy shoes."

"Her family probably made a generous donation to the university so they would drop the charges. We can't prove it, so let it go, Paige. Be happy you've got your life back."

The justice system sucked!

* * * * *

Determined, Danny pushed himself to walk across the room without the aid of his cane. He had only managed to get two-thirds of the way, when his leg gave out and he crumpled to the floor in an impotent heap.

Grimacing, he fought the pain as he struggled to his feet. His knees felt like they'd been whacked with a baseball bat. Flame licked at his bad thigh.

Rubber-soled shoes sucked at the floor like a demon seconds before strong arms lifted him from behind. "You trying to kill yourself on my watch, Captain? Destroy my excellent record?"

"Just trying to walk like a man." He hated admitting defeat but couldn't hide the too-obvious fact. He had fallen like a house built on the sand.

"Orderlies! I need assistance over here," the Air Force nurse called. She tsk-tsked as she held him upright. "The ability to walk doesn't make someone a man. The sooner you get that into your thick head, the better off you'll be."

"Because I may never walk normally again?" He'd have a gimpy gait like an old warhorse? Or worse, he'd wind up confined to a wheelchair.

Two husky young men clad in hospital whites flanked him and lifted him onto one of the cots in the physical therapy room. Like the nurse thought Adonis and Hercules here would help him? Next to these hulks he felt like less than a ninety-eight pound weakling.

"No, Sir. There are lots of physically fit males around but a lot of them don't qualify as men in my book. That special something comes from your heart and soul."

Danny stared at the nurse long and hard, pillowing his head on his arms. She made a lot of sense, even if it was a dig at his down-and-out attitude.

Penny breezed in, her wrists and ankles jangling from a profusion of shiny bracelets. "Hello, darling. I thought I'd find you running laps."

Danny bit back a snarl. He twisted around awkwardly to look at his uninvited visitor and said with a sour note in his voice, "You're a long way from home."

"Biloxi is *our* home," she reminded him with a "silly boy" tone of voice that irked him. Sidling up to him, she looked slinky, almost sleazy, in her silk shift. "Can't I come down to the coast to see my favorite man?"

"Favorite man?" Last time he had checked, she'd dumped him and had Matt Conrath's baby. They'd maintained a tenuous friendship but calling him her *favorite man* was pretty far-fetched. "What do you want, Pen?"

She rubbed his back, taking liberties she'd forfeited long ago. "Just some commiseration."

Paige must've made her accusations public against Penny.

Penny pouted prettily and twisted her hair around her finger. "I'm sure you've heard all the vile muckety muck she's spreading around about me."

Not much but curious, he watched and listened closely. "What's your side of the story?"

Penny shuffled her feet and hung her head, her bouncy curls framing her suddenly flaming cheeks. "I borrowed a teensy bit of money from the store but I've replaced it and made amends. The university's not going to press charges and I still get to graduate."

Danny shook his head to clear his ears. Penny had stolen the money? Whoa! His radar was way off.

She rushed on, her voice breathy, her eyes imploring. "But I had the best of reasons. I couldn't let my poor baby starve or go without a roof over her head, now could I? What kind of mama would that make me?"

Penny was so desperate she had to steal to feed her kid? "Why didn't you ask me for help instead of taking that money?"

"You were a little far away." She averted her gaze from him and her full black lashes swept her high cheekbones. "Besides, I was jealous of Paige, what with you taking up with her and all and I wasn't sure how friendly you felt toward me any more."

He hadn't felt especially friendly toward her since she'd dumped him so callously.

So Penny had set up Paige. Why wasn't he surprised? "And you were jealous enough to make it look like Paige stole the money?" He knew the answer but wanted to hear it from her lips.

She clasped his hand between both of his and dragged it up to her lips. "I'm not proud of myself, but yes. When I noticed she signed off on the books a couple days when it wasn't right, and I was so very desperate, I let it look like it was still her error. She's been so terribly spiteful to me, flaunting you in my face, making nasty digs, she deserved a comeuppance."

Fury raged in his veins. Of all the conniving things to do. Seething, he could barely stand to look at her. She had done him a huge favor by dumping him.

When Danny remained silent, Penny stroked the stray hair off his forehead, her fingertips light, trying to be seductive, but dismally missing the mark. "Don't."

Pain pooled in Penny's eyes as she pulled back her hand. "I know now it was wrong and I regret my actions but haven't I been punished enough? I've lost my job in the bookstore and I have to hock my jewelry to buy food for my dear little Annemarie. Is there any hope for us? I readily admit that I made a dreadful mistake. I still love you."

He didn't love her. He no longer even liked her. He inventoried the desperate and misguided woman pleading for another chance. As outwardly exquisite as she was with her honey-gold tresses and alabaster complexion, she was a barren wasteland inside. She didn't know right from wrong or seem to recollect that she'd become pregnant with another man's child as soon as he went off to war. The other man should marry her if he had one grain of honor. "No, Penny. There's no hope."

"You wanted to marry me. Surely you still love me, at least a little bit. We were so good together, remember?"

A growl rose in his throat. "Obviously not good enough." The blinding rage of her betrayal long since dissipated, only disgust remained. He retrieved his hand and regarded her icily.

Gray bitterness crept over her finely etched features, contorting them. "I suppose you're going to run back to Paige and make up?"

Precisely. He remained stoic, regarding her soberly. He loved Paige. He wasn't sure he had ever loved the woman standing in front of him, making excuses for her dishonorable actions.

"You should rethink that. That one has a heart of pure granite. She wants to press charges against me, and have me rot in that musty old jail while my poor baby gets put in foster care. Nor does she want me to be allowed to graduate. Is that the kind of vengeful woman you want?" She flounced across the room, her shoulder bag slapping her backside.

Danny wanted to howl his outrage but he kept his voice very quiet and level. "No. That's not the kind of woman I want and why I'm glad you're out of my life. What kind of mercy did you show Paige when you left her to rot in jail? To get kicked out of college?"

Penny's mouth moved but no sound came out. All color drained from her face and she swayed ever so slightly.

"Goodbye, Penny. Nurse! I'm late for an important appointment." This time he'd hear Paige out whether she liked it or not. And she would listen to what he had to say as well.

* * * * *

Paige sauntered out of class into the bright April sunshine. Already sweltering at eleven a.m., heat shimmered up from the tarmac and the grass wilted as if gasping for air. It'd be another iced-tea summer. A scorcher, the temps would most probably climb into the triple digits.

She hitched her books more securely into the crook of her arm as she debated amiably with a couple of fellow students headed in the same direction. Then she saw Danny and stopped dead in mid-sentence, mid-road, her heart lodged in her throat.

Danny lounged against a Mimosa tree in front of the Delta Pi house, his arms crossed over his chest, a walking cane leaning against his leg. Was he a mirage? Surely he wouldn't truly be here. At least not for her.

Only when a car honked at her and the driver yelled obscenities out the window, did she awaken from her stupor. While one part of her wanted to throw herself into Danny's arms, the other part wanted to keep on walking and pretend she hadn't recognized him.

All the hurt of his betrayal flooded back, along with Penny's confession that Danny was her little girl's father.

Ordering her hormones to behave, she decided to face him. She'd look far more foolish running away. Much better to act the mature sophisticate and pretend he was nothing more than her brother's friend.

"What are you doing here?" *So cool!* She wanted to bite her gauche tongue.

"No, you." Danny pushed himself away from the ancient tree and ambled toward her only leaning slightly on his cane. Despite her anger at the man, she was pleased to see him making progress.

Why would he be here to see her? Did he know the truth? Did he want to apologize? Or did he want to chew her out again?

"Can we talk?" He made his way to the picnic tables outside the Business building and lowered himself to a weathered bench.

"About what?" She remained standing in case she wanted to make a fast getaway after all. Her shadow stretched out behind her, as if it wanted a head start.

"Your case. Penny filled me in on her side."

Paige blinked. *Penny must have given him an earful.* The woman had been gloating about getting away with murder and still blamed herself for all her woes. No doubt Penny would have justified her actions to anyone who would listen. "Well bless her soul."

"I had a lucky escape from her."

What? She couldn't have heard right. Her full attention riveted on him. "What do you mean?"

He ran a fingertip down her arm, making her shiver. "I mean, I'm glad she's out of my life. I don't think I ever knew her. She's definitely not a woman I want to know."

So was this all he wanted to tell her? That he was through with Penny? She waited for him to say more, wishing with all her heart he would stop torturing her. The way the Mississippi sun kissed his sun-bleached hair and the gentle breeze whipped it across his forehead made her long to reach out and stroke it away from his face and play with it. But she didn't dare until she knew exactly why he was here. "Why have you come?"

"I'm in love with you and I want you back." Danny stood and closed in on her, staring at her intently, making her insides quake.

Paige's throat constricted and her pulse fluttered in her neck. *"You love me?"* she asked after several rapidly tattooing heartbeats, her eyes wide.

Cupping her cheek in his palm, he caressed the contours with his calloused thumb, and gazed deeply into her eyes. "You're my sun, moon and stars. It's time I deal with my injury and get on with my life. It's time I stop pushing you away and start supporting you the way you were there for me when I needed you. "

Awestruck, giddiness stole her breath. *Danny loved her!* She wanted to fling herself into his arms but that would have to wait. She just thanked God he was home and safe on the road to recovery and that, finally, all the enemy fire had ceased for them both, domestic and abroad.

She settled for tippy-toeing up to him and placing a soft kiss on his lips. She took his hands in hers and gazed deeply into his smoldering eyes. "I love you, too. It's time we support each other."

He lowered his lips to hers and parted them forcefully with a red-hot kiss. When he finally released them, he let out a war whoop, startling her.

Still, the fateful threesome plagued her mind and she needed reassurance that he didn't wish a repeat. "Will I be enough to satisfy you?"

"Yes, yes and yes." A wicked gleam twinkled in his eyes. "You're all I ever need or want. I should tie you up and spank you for ever doubting that."

"Ooh, please do!" Eager to try some bondage, she squirmed against him, exhilarated at the naughty image he was creating in her mind.

When her old, staid professor passed by them, gaping, she couldn't suppress the sunny smile teasing her lips. "He loves me," she said simply, hugging her soldier blissfully.

Danny chuckled heartily, leaning his forehead against hers, his breath scorching her face. "I wasn't teasing."

Her pussy tingling, she nibbled his ear and whispered huskily, "I hope not. When can I cash in?"

He traced her lower lip with the pad of his thumb. "Just as soon as we can find the closest bed."

She wiggled her eyebrows at him and her nipples puckered, pushing out against the thin fabric of her cotton polo shirt. "Good thing I ordered some toys from hotsex.com."

"Toys?" Twin patches of color brightened his cheeks, his brows arched and he laced his fingers through hers, squeezing her hand.

Charmed that such a macho man could react so virginally to the mention of sex toys, she treated him to her sauciest smile. "Some very naughty, wonderful toys guaranteed to turn you on."

"You turn me on." His khakis stretching tightly across the tight ridge of his desire had already clued her in that he was hot for her. But she didn't object to hearing him murmur the husky words.

If they didn't find a bed soon, she was liable to ravage him right here he was making her so hot.

"We've got to get a place of our own—immediately." He nuzzled her neck, making it impossible to breath.

"Have mercy." She arched her neck to give him better access. His moist warm lips felt so wonderful, she moaned.

"No mercy," he murmured against the pulse point of her throat, thrilling her. "You're all mine now."

She loved the sound of that. And he was all hers.

He led the way to his car, walking faster and steadier. "You're good therapy."

A grin split her face and she said on a chuckle, "You're just horny."

"I'm in love. Seems sex is the therapy I needed all along." His fiery glance almost made her burst out in flame.

"If that's the case, I'm prepared to give you *lots* of *therapy*."

"Keep up that dirty talk and I'll take you right here in the car."

She was ready to let him. Instead, she cajoled in a singsong voice, "Tia's in class all day. We have the house to ourselves."

"I'd rather we go to my hotel, so we have all day *and all night*." He rubbed her hand, lying on the seat between them, heating her flesh.

She was easy. She was a raging inferno. She linked her fingers through his joining with him in the only safe way possible while he was driving. "Just stop at the house so I can get the handcuffs."

"You got any whipped cream?" He winked at her broadly and the telltale heat crept up her neck and settled into the apples of her cheeks.

"I'll see what I can wrangle up." *Uhm…whipped cream and handcuffs.* Her mouth watered deliciously, anticipating the taste of his salty flesh topped by the creamy concoction.

She gathered up her toys and toppings and rejoined Danny lickety-split, afraid he really was a mirage that would disappear the minute she turned her back on him. But he was there, wearing a crooked grin that made her knees go weak, when she emerged from the house.

"I missed you." He dragged her into his arms and drank deeply of her lips, his hands roaming her back. It was a wonder her clothing didn't spontaneously combust from their heat.

She hoped and prayed she'd never have to miss him again. Against his lips, she asked, "You won't have to return to Iraq, will you?"

"Not with this bum leg. I'm short enough to jump off a dime." When she gave him a dumb look, he added, "That means I'm being discharged as we speak." Sadness tinged his voice, catching her by surprise.

Her forehead furrowed as she tried to figure out the mystery of this many-faceted man. "You want to go back?"

He pulled her into his arms, his heart beating strongly against hers. Nuzzling the top of her head, he murmured, "No, baby. I'm right where I want to be for the rest of my life—right in your arms. But I don't like the reason I can't go back and I'll miss the guys in my unit. I didn't get to say goodbye."

Warmed by his revelation, she snuggled closer against his heart. She had always dreamed he would be her life mate but to have him echo her most heart-felt desire made her tingly all over. "Maybe you can write to them, see them when they return?"

"Yeah." Gazing down into her eyes deeply, he squeezed her gently. "Sounds like a plan."

She rubbed against him sensually and murmured against his neck seductively, "The quicker we get to your hotel, the faster I can take your mind off everything but me."

Primitive growls rumbled in his chest and he set her away from him on her side of the car. What seemed a heartbeat later, they were inside Danny's room and he was putting a blindfold over her eyes and making sure she couldn't see anything. He coaxed her to lift her arms high over her head, he pulled her shirt over her head and dropped it on the floor. A moment later he buried his face between her breasts as he unlatched the tiny front hooks of her bra and let it slide off her shoulders.

She squirmed, his tongue exhilarating her, sweeping under her heavy globes and swirling around in smaller and smaller circles until it lapped the tight little bud of her aching nipple. His unshaven jaw tickled, ever slightly so raspy and ultra-masculine against her soft flesh. She arched against him, pushing her breast into his mouth, greedy for him to suckle her.

Instead, he nipped it with his teeth, and then trailed a fiery path down her belly, stopping at the waistband of her jeans. Deftly, he slipped the button from its hole and lowered her coverings so that they pooled at her feet. Following with his tongue, he licked the inside of her quivering thighs but steered clear of her mons, much to her chagrin.

"Lay down on the bed," he ordered huskily as he licked his way down to her knees.

In a daze from the full-scale assault on her senses, she did as bade, letting her legs hang over the edge to give him easy access to her.

"No darling, all the way back."

Unsure how much more she could stand, she scooted back on the mattress as he commanded. Fur tickled her ankle and then encircled it, making her shiver with anticipation.

"Spread your legs wide."

She licked her lips, liking the sound of that.

"Wider," he implored and then she heard a second loud click and presumed he had fastened her leg to the bedpost. To test her theory, she tugged at it, only to be yanked back. Excitement and anticipation thrummed through her veins. *Sure enough, he had cuffed her to the bed.*

For all her big talk of wanting to be tied up, this was her first experience and she shuddered deliciously. Danny was in complete control now and his warning of no mercy flashed through her mind.

A second handcuff caught her other ankle to the far post. She expected him to cuff her wrists next but instead he suckled her big toe and massaged her foot. He licked each toe in turn, then flickered his tongue over her instep, tickling her unmercifully.

"Stop!" she pleaded, giggling, straining to sit up. Though her hands were free, she couldn't manage a stomach crunch with her legs spread so far apart. Frustrated, she yanked her feet to no avail, the cuffs holding strong.

"No you don't, baby." Danny's tongue stopped ministering to her feet, her soles suddenly chilly from the loss of his moist warmth.

She heard suspicious jangling and then he clasped her wrist gently. "Lay still."

More fur caressed her wrist and then he stretched her arm high above her head and chained it to the headboard. Straddling her, his swollen cock teasing her belly, he tied her other hand to the bed so that she was truly captive.

Writhing, testing the strength of her bonds, she assured herself she was truly at his mercy. She licked her lips in anticipation of his next move. Whipped cream, she hoped.

Instead, something light and airy touched her nose. Then it glided down her throat to her breasts.

A feather!

She squirmed as it caressed its way down to her mons, to her inner thigh, finally stopping on her clit. So light, so whispery, so soft, it was pure, excruciating torture. Rapture well on its way, her juices flowed readily.

"You like that?"

She nodded, her thoughts jumbling as wild sensations mounted unbearably. "Um…"

He dusted her entire body with the giant plume and then went all quiet for a few seconds. Panic set in. *Would he leave her tied to a bed?* "Danny?"

Again she expected him to start with her breasts and go down on her. Instead, he applied the whipped cream generously onto her mons and buried his face between her legs ravenously, like a starved man.

In no time, he had devoured the whipped cream and lapped her juices, turning her inside out with white-hot desire. He suckled her labia and then her clitoris as he stroked first one, then two fingers in and out of her.

Exquisite pressure mounted inside her and she was about to be consumed by a raging fireball when he suddenly lifted himself away at the crucial moment.

"Not yet, baby." He crawled up her length and laid atop her, pressing her deeper into the mattress, nestling his searing cock between her legs, but still not seeking entry.

One huge, raging hormone, she rubbed against him, thrusting her hips at him.

The devil incarnate ignored her and latched onto her breast, pulling it deeply into his mouth. Then he trailed fiery kisses to its mate.

She squirmed and writhed but his cock still teased her, against her but, unmercifully, not entering her.

Her head spinning, her heart aching with raw desire, she pleaded, "Fuck me."

"How bad do you want it?" He rubbed the velvety slick tip of his cock across her labia, overwhelming her with the sudden swirl of sensations.

"So badly I'm going to burst if I don't have it."

"Not without me, babe." He thrust into her so deeply, she yelped. His penetration stretched her, completed her and they were as one moving together. He captured her lips and their tongues mated as he plunged deeper and deeper into her, each stroke flooding her with another wave of rapture.

Every inch of her flesh blazed with fire. She clenched his cock tightly, milking it greedily. Intoxicated, she gave herself up to the wondrous love swelling in her chest, drinking as deeply of him as he did of her.

His rhythm increased and he stroked in and out wildly. He released her lips and gulped air into his lungs as he pushed himself up on his arms for greater leverage for one final, powerful thrust.

Crescendoing with him, she sheathed his cock tightly in her velvety folds, her hips thrust high and the muscles in her upper legs corded. Monumental explosions rocketed through her, propelling her to the heavens so that she floated on clouds of ecstasy.

Danny rolled off her and nuzzled her lips. "I'm addicted to you. I can't get enough." He began kissing her again, but this time, light, individual kisses in an odd pattern of sorts.

"What are you doing?" Curious, she cursed the blindfold that robbed her of the sight of her lover.

His voice dropped to a seductive growl. "Connecting the dots. Every last one of them."

"We'll be here all night!" Goose bumps rising on her arms, she thrilled to the idea, not merely making peace with her freckles, but embracing them.

"Later. Right now we're going to the beach."

Stunned, she lay still despite the turbulent emotions overpowering her. The Biloxi beaches lay two hours south by car. *"Now?"*

He uncuffed her and removed the blindfold. "Now, darlin'," he drawled seductively.

Stretching her achy muscles, she was very aware of his heated, still passionate gaze devouring her.

Mystified, she showered and dressed wondering if she had somehow disappointed him. "Why are we going to the beach?"

A secretive, seductive smile curved his cheek. "You'll find out."

Blanketed by the star-filled night, they rode in silence as he munched on a string of red licorice. As they approached the Gulf shore, a balmy, shrimp-scented breeze caressed her through the open windows, whipping her long hair across her face. *Home sweet home.* Tucking her unruly mane behind her ears, she almost purred her delight to be home. God she hadn't realized 'til just this moment how homesick she'd been.

The middle of the night by now, the streets of Biloxi and Gulfport were nearly devoid of traffic. Only when Danny pulled his car onto Highway 90, the beach drive, did they run across the remnants of the coast's nightlife. Tall casinos cast cool shadows over them as they drove by, their late night lounges pumping out sultry New Orleans style jazz.

Danny parked near the pier where they had gone crabbing as kids and swam in the warm Gulf waters. He opened her door and offered her a helping hand from the car.

Wistfully, she eyed the murky water, breathtaking memories assailing her. "We going crabbing?"

Danny bestowed an adoring smile on her that made her glow warmly inside. "Not quite."

"Swimming?" Crabbing in knee-deep water was one thing. Swimming in the murky depths was a dangerous proposition she wasn't about to attempt.

"Nope." He turned and clasped both her hands, pulling her onto her beloved beach.

He wasn't up for a stroll yet so what was he thinking? She bit her lower lip to stop from blurting out her thoughts, which she knew he wouldn't appreciate, and busied herself kicking off her shoes and letting the cool sand trickle through her toes.

"Let's sit awhile and watch the shrimp boats. I've really missed coming here." Nostalgia filled his voice as he gazed lovingly out across the dark Gulf as his thumb caressed her knuckles as he held her hand in his.

They sat companionably for a few silent moments, listening to the lazy lap of ocean waves washing up against the shore. Languidly, she started to build a castle and make a pile of pretty shells she found while sifting through the damp sand. "I've missed Biloxi, too." *What an understatement!* Pangs of homesickness washed over her and she longed to stay for far longer than just a brief interlude.

Danny stretched out on the beach and drew a picture in the sand with his forefinger. It took shape of a hangman's noose and several blank lines beneath. "Guess a letter."

She took a double take at the child's game staring her in the face. *He wanted to play hangman? Now?* Simple pleasures obviously amused him but she would have thought he would have wanted to do something a little more fun. A little more risqué.

Okay, she was game. If it made him happy. She just enjoyed being with him, whatever they were doing. She always started with vowels as every word had to have at least one and the odds were in her favor. " 'A'."

"He wrote an 'A' on the second blank line and applauded her, mischief dancing in his eyes.

Intrigued, she pursed her lips and considered her strategy. "Give me an 'E'."

He wrote an 'E' on the last blank line. "You're good at this."

She glowed inside at the meaningless compliment.

"What next?"

" 'S'."

He made a buzzer sound. "Wrong." He drew a circle for the head. "Try again."

She tapped a finger to her lips. There were two words, five blanks in the first word and two blanks in the second word. " 'T'."

He screwed up his lips and drew a long line for the poor soul's body. "Nope. Again."

Cramped, she shifted around and crossed her legs Indian style. Leaning over the puzzling blanks, she pondered them.

"Take your time, but remember it'll be daylight in four hours." Mirth danced in his devilish eyes.

Irked, she stuck out her tongue at him and play punched the smart aleck in his brawny shoulder. " 'B'."

"I take it back. You're lousy at this." With a wily expression, he drew an arm with a flourish and tossed her a sly grin. "Try again."

Perplexed both by the game and his demeanor, she reverted back to her safest bet—another vowel. " 'I'."

He shook his head and drew the second foot with a flourish. "Come on, college girl. Surely you can figure it out."

With only two tries left and twenty letters left in the alphabet? *Yeah. Right.* " 'R'."

He wrote two 'R's and clapped, bestowing a proud but challenging smile on her. "You're still in the game."

Staring at the letters, her eyes crossed, her equilibrium way off-kilter. Her blood humming fast and furiously through her veins, she swallowed hard and prayed she wasn't dreaming. *It couldn't be!*

After several heart-stopping moments, she sucked in much needed air and ordered her heart to start beating again. "'M'."

Headlights from a passing car on the beach highway illuminating him, he wrote not one but two 'M's, one at the beginning of each word, and then gazed soulfully into her eyes. "Do you know the answer?" His sultry, husky voice was calibrated for seduction.

From the moment she'd met him. "Yes!" Joyfully, she flung her arms around him and they rolled over in the sand until he lay on top of her, his heart hammering against hers.

He rubbed her nose with his. "I think I just lost the ring in the sand, rolling around like two randy teenagers."

Alarmed that her ring would be found by some smarmy kid with a metal detector and forever lost to her, she wriggled out from under his delicious weight. "No ring, no marriage," she teased, but searched desperately on her hands and knees anyway, looking for a glint of moonlight to illuminate the precious gold band.

He tapped her on the shoulder, his touch electrifying her more than any live wire could. "Stand up and turn around."

Dare she? Did she dare not? Sandy and gritty, she pivoted on the ball of her foot and came face to face with a ring-sized blue velvet container. She gulped as her gaze fixated on the velvet box.

He had situated himself on one knee and gazed up at her raptly, making her heart climb in her throat. "Marry me."

"With or without the ring." *Biloxi or no Biloxi.* But she wasn't about to admit the second confession just yet. She'd been granted all her wishes so far and maybe she'd get another one. With a contented sigh, she gave up on keeping her hair from tangling in the ocean breeze that whipped it around her face.

"Always and forever." Danny slipped the band of gold on her finger, and then stood. He cupped her face in the palms of his warm hands and rubbed his calloused thumbs across the line of her cheeks, his warm breath feathering across her blazing cheeks. Pure yearning slammed through her an instant before his greedy, all-consuming and oh-so-wonderful kiss brought her to her knees under the capricious Biloxi moon.

The End

Enjoy this excerpt from

American Beauty

Sticky & Sweet

© Copyright Ashley Ladd, 2003

He must've dozed off, for he awoke with a start when silky hair caressed his cheek and a lace-covered breast grazed his arm. "Wake up, Sleeping Beauty," a very sultry, husky voice crooned. "I brought home your favorite – Prime Rib and chocolate covered strawberries." She perched on the couch beside him, leaning over him, her creamy breasts almost falling out of a slinky, frilly creation he was sure was illegal throughout the First World.

Had he thought of her as a sprite? Temptress was more like it. No, *siren* was the apt description. Those dusky aureoles peaked out at him again and his blood pressure shot sky high.

He swallowed hard, his pulse hammering and his breathing uneven. His cock sprung to full attention. He knew he should move away, make a joke, or do something to diffuse the dangerous situation, but he couldn't. Not when she scooted back and rubbed against him, torturing him inhumanely.

She smelled of lilacs, vanilla, and strawberries. Then he realized it was an oddly smoky vanilla scent, and fresh juicy strawberries. He pried his gaze from her tight nipples and noticed for the first time how the dim lights flickered from candles on every surface. "Is it my birthday?" His voice crackled, sultrier than hers. His cock ached to get out of his palace and play. *Down boy!* It had only suffered a female drought for a few days, not the eon it felt like.

Kirsty licked her shiny lips, slow and languorously, her pink tongue just peeking out those luscious lips, promising pleasure beyond compare to any man brave enough to take up her invitation. And she undoubtedly invited him. But why? Until tonight, she'd been sweet and teetered on the shy side. Why had she morphed into this voluptuous seductress who knew all the moves, and flaunted her voluptuous body in sucking distance, to drive him so wild to forget himself and his mission?

Stars twinkled in her eyes and she ran a fingernail down his chest, which she let hover just below his navel, at the snap of his jeans. Her nipples strained against the see-through lace, taut little buds teasing him unmercifully.

He longed to touch the outer rim of her dusky areole, and his mouth went dry. He could taste it deep inside his mouth.

"What do you want for your birthday?" She leaned over him, and her bodice gaped open to give him a nearly full view of the gorgeous breast.

He sucked in his breath unable to tear his gaze from the perfect view. When she sat down again, rubbing against him, his shaft strained to be free. He didn't know how much more torture he could stand. Never had he restrained himself before and he could barely remember why he needed to now. The female was not only willing, she was begging him to fuck her.

"Hungry?"

He almost fell off the couch, but rolled into her instead, increasing his pain to even more excruciating levels. "Starved," he admitted, hoping she didn't plan to tease and torture him all night like this. If she seduced him, as she surely seemed to be doing, he could succumb. Even Crowe couldn't fault a red-blooded man for being unable to resist the lures of a nearly naked seductress.

"In that case," a slow smile dawned over her face making her glow, "Open your mouth wide. I have something special for you."

Enjoy this excerpt from
Carbon Copy
© Copyright Ashley Ladd, 2004

Rough, the guard chained Siobhan's hands behind her back, clasped a metal ring around her neck, and hauled her like a dog to death's corridor. The heavy chain clanked on the floor, biting into her neck and making it almost impossible to hold her head up. With every scrap of strength she could muster, she held it up to meet her fate head on, marching proudly past the rows of the worst deviants and *slogs* in the galaxy.

"What'd you do, sweet thing? Burn the muffins?" A particularly disgusting double-faced, four-legged Glitopuss taunted, coiling his long slimy tongue toward her. His genitals swelled and glistened grotesquely in the *weblinthium's* pulsing glow.

She veiled her eyes, looking away. Unfortunately, the view was no better wherever her glance fell.

"Maybe the Diva Goddess stuck that perky nose up in the air at the King," a single-breasted Pretadorn drawled. Sporting a single beady eye and three nostrils, she was as abominable as the Glitopuss.

"You take a wrong turn? The debutante ball is in the penthouse, at the top of the compound." Startled by the svelte, human voice, her gaze sought out the owner. He appeared to be the only man on the corridor. The inmate's amused gaze dissected each and every inch of her. He leaned against the *weblinthium* bars nonchalantly as if he was hanging out at the cantina. Mischief danced in the man's jade eyes, striking against his waist-length coal-black hair. He was simultaneously the most disreputable and sexiest male she'd ever seen, so much so, he made her forget to breathe. "Don't mind them. They never heard of manners."

And he had? Regardless of his handsome façade, she detected no evidence of his so-called manners. "You're on death's corridor because you have such sterling ones?" Siobhan returned the favor, letting her gaze drink him in. Tall enough to make her look up at him, the man had to stand at least six foot four inches. Broad shoulders tapered down to a narrow waist, slim hips, and powerful legs. Mocking intelligence smoldered in his disturbing gaze. Unkempt though he was, she grudgingly admitted the man was ruggedly handsome, with sculpted cheeks, a braided beard with faded beads strung through the two braids, and a high forehead, which his unruly locks insisted on tumbling over. He was one-hundred-eighty degrees opposite her fiancé's polished blonde figure. He wore the outfit of pirates, her sworn enemies.

"Just a little misunderstanding, sweet thing. My *attorneys* are working on my *appeal* as we speak."

Sweet thing? Hardly. If he'd heard the rumors of her supposed crime, he wouldn't waste a drop of charm on her. "Hope your attorneys are better than mine." Considering her own case, it was possible, if highly unlikely, he spoke the truth. Danger seeped from his every pore, mixed in with his scallywag charm. Charming men made her internal alarms whir out of control—they couldn't be trusted. Her father had tried to alliance her with several. Blatantly honest, she loved her straightforward Dennis. No artifice. No games. Thoroughly trustworthy, she could consign him her life. She had done so often and he had never let her down.

So where was he now?

Trying to find her, most definitely. She had been captured and arrested without due process…

The guard disabled the *weblinthium* force field in the cell across from the pirate, then unclasped the chain from her collar and shoved her inside. In a reverberating, mechanical voice, he said, "Better pray fast to your gods. Your execution will be at the rise of the third Balderian moon."

About the author:

Ashley Ladd lives in South Florida with her husband, five children, and beloved pets. She loves the water, animals (especially cats), and playing on the computer.

She's been told she has a wicked sense of humor and often incorporates humor and adventure into her books. She also adores very spicy romance which she also weaves into her stories.

Ashley Ladd welcomes mail from readers. You can write to her c/o Ellora's Cave Publishing at 1056 Home Avenue, Akron OH 44310-3502.

Why an electronic book?

We live in the Information Age — an exciting time in the history of human civilization in which technology rules supreme and continues to progress in leaps and bounds every minute of every hour of every day. For a multitude of reasons, more and more avid literary fans are opting to purchase e-books instead of paperbacks. The question to those not yet initiated to the world of electronic reading is simply: *why?*

1. *Price.* An electronic title at Ellora's Cave Publishing runs anywhere from 40-75% less than the cover price of the <u>exact same title</u> in paperback format. Why? Cold mathematics. It is less expensive to publish an e-book than it is to publish a paperback, so the savings are passed along to the consumer.

2. *Space.* Running out of room to house your paperback books? That is one worry you will never have with electronic novels. For a low one-time cost, you can purchase a handheld computer designed specifically for e-reading purposes. Many e-readers are larger than the average handheld, giving you plenty of screen room. Better yet, hundreds of titles can be stored within your new library — a single microchip. (Please note that Ellora's Cave does not endorse any specific brands. You can check our website at www.ellorascave.com for customer recommendations we make available to new consumers.)

3. *Mobility.* Because your new library now consists of only a microchip, your entire cache of books can be taken with you wherever you go.

4. *Personal preferences are accounted for.* Are the words you are currently reading too small? Too large? Too...ANNOYING? Paperback books cannot be modified according to personal preferences, but e-books can.

5. *Innovation.* The way you read a book is not the only advancement the Information Age has gifted the literary community with. There is also the factor of what you can read. Ellora's Cave Publishing will be introducing a new line of interactive titles that are available in e-book format only.

6. *Instant gratification.* Is it the middle of the night and all the bookstores are closed? Are you tired of waiting days—sometimes weeks—for online and offline bookstores to ship the novels you bought? Ellora's Cave Publishing sells instantaneous downloads 24 hours a day, 7 days a week, 365 days a year. Our e-book delivery system is 100% automated, meaning your order is filled as soon as you pay for it.

Those are a few of the top reasons why electronic novels are displacing paperbacks for many an avid reader. As always, Ellora's Cave Publishing welcomes your questions and comments. We invite you to email us at service@ellorascave.com or write to us directly at: 1056 Home Avenue, Akron OH 44310-3502.

NEED A MORE EXCITING
WAY TO PLAN YOUR DAY?

ELLORA'S
CAVEMEN
2006 CALENDAR

COMING THIS FALL

THE
ELLORA'S CAVE
LIBRARY

Stay up to date with Ellora's Cave Titles
in Print with our Quarterly Catalog.

TO RECIEVE A CATALOG,
SEND AN EMAIL WITH YOUR NAME
AND MAILING ADDRESS TO:

CATALOG@ELLORASCAVE.COM

OR SEND A LETTER OR POSTCARD
WITH YOUR MAILING ADDRESS TO:
CATALOG REQUEST
C/O ELLORA'S CAVE PUBLISHING, INC.
1337 COMMERCE DRIVE #13
STOW, OH 44224

Lady *Jaided* Regular Features

Jaid's Tirade
Jaid Black's erotic romance novels sell throughout the world, and her publishing company Ellora's Cave is one of the largest and most successful e-book publishers in the world. What is less well known about Jaid Black, a.k.a. Tina Engler is her long record as a political activist. Whether she's discussing sex or politics (or both), expect to see her get up on her soapbox and do what she does best: offend the greedy, the holier-than-thous, and the apathetic! Don't miss out on her monthly column.

Devilish Dot's G-Spot
Married to the same man for 20 years, Dorothy Araiza still basks in a sex life to be envied. What Dot loves just as much as achieving the Big O is helping other women realize their full sexual potential. Dot gives talks and advice on everything from which sex toys to buy (or not to buy) to which positions give you the best climax.

On the Road with Lady K
Publisher, author, world traveler and Lady of Barrow, Kathryn Falk shares insider information on the most romantic places in the world.

Kandidly Kay
This Lois Lane cum Dave Barry is a domestic goddess by day and a hard-hitting sexual deviancy reporter by night. Adored for her stunning wit and knack for delivering one-liners, this Rodney Dangerfield of reporting will leave no stone unturned in her search for the bizarre truth.

A Model World
CJ Hollenbach returns to his roots. The blond heartthrob from Ohio has twice been seen in Playgirl magazine and countless other publications. He has appeared on several national TV shows including The Jerry Springer Show (God help him!) and has been interviewed for Entertainment Tonight, CNN and The Today Show. He has been involved in the romance industry for the past 12 years, appearing on dozens of romance novel covers and calendars. CJ's specialty is personal interviews, in which people have a tendency to tell him everything.

Hot Mama Cooks
Sex is her food, and food is her sex. Hot Mama gives aphrodisiac a whole new meaning. Join her every month for her latest sensual adventure -- with bonus recipe!

Empress on the Mount
Brash, outrageous, and undeniably irreverent, this advice columnist from down under will either leave you in stitches or recovering from hang-jaw as you gawk at her answers to reader questions on relationships and life.

Erotic Fiction from Ellora's Cave
The debut issue will feature part one of "Ferocious," a three-part erotic serial written especially for Lady Jaided by the popular Sherri L. King.

Discover for yourself why readers can't get enough of the multiple award-winning publisher Ellora's Cave. Whether you prefer e-books or paperbacks, be sure to visit EC on the web at www.ellorascave.com for an erotic reading experience that will leave you breathless.

www.ellorascave.com